What You Get at Home

What You Get at Home

by Dora Dueck

TURNSTONE PRESS

Turnstone Press
Artspace Building
206-100 Arthur Street
Winnipeg, MB
R3B 1H3 Canada
www.TurnstonePress.com

Several stories from this collection have appeared, often in slightly different versions, in the following magazines and anthologies: *Prairie Fire* ("My Name Is Magdalena" and "Helping Isaak"), *Center for Mennonite Writing* ("Chopsticks"), *Room* ("Postponement"), *Rhubarb* ("White"), *Direction* ("Patricia Beach"), and *Journal of Mennonite Studies,* reprinted in *Sophia* ("Crucifix on the Road to Gnadenheim").

Turnstone Press gratefully acknowledges the assistance of the Canada Council for the Arts, the Manitoba Arts Council, the Government of Canada through the Canada Book Fund, and the Province of Manitoba through the Book Publishing Tax Credit and the Book Publisher Marketing Assistance Program.

Printed and bound in Canada by Friesens for Turnstone Press.

Library and Archives Canada Cataloguing in Publication

Dueck, Dora, 1950-

    What you get at home / Dora Dueck.

ISBN 978-0-88801-404-7

    I. Title.

PS8557.U2813W42 2012   C813'.54   C2012-904935-2

Contents

with thanks
to my parents,
Tina and the late Peter J. Doerksen

What You Get at Home

Chopsticks

The year I was eleven and Danny was ten, our parents enrolled us in piano lessons with a woman named Mrs. Jackson, who lived in the next town over. She was plump and careless, and perhaps the only person in the area available to teach us. Even as a child, new to the instrument, I realized the limitations of her musical gifts. She laughed a great deal and seemed to clamour over the keys.

Each week after Mrs. Jackson had exhausted our lessons before their allotted time, she showed off at the piano while we watched *I Love Lucy* or *The Three Stooges* on a television in the adjoining room. Her performances were show tunes, I think, and reminded me of kittens tangled in string.

I was learning simple melodies, one hand first, then two; learning my notes, time values, sharps and flats. Mrs. Jackson said my fingers were talented but I ignored her praise, and dreamed when I practised of the pieces my father played on his records. Of their intelligence, their anguish. He liked classical music and though I had never seen the ocean, except in pictures, I felt that his music was like the sea, variously stormy or still. But I never let on that I was listening, never asked for titles or composers, as if his albums were adult conversations that would stop mid-beat if he discovered I was eavesdropping.

We took the lessons on Thursdays after school. My father was a teacher at the high school in town, and Thursdays he pulled up to the elementary school in our big white Chevrolet, grinning like he was thrilled to see us again, and Danny and I sprang out of the clump of students waiting for the bus, me with a head's toss as if I'd just won a prize that everyone wanted, and we bounded away on the ten-mile drive south along the tracks. Neither Danny nor I enjoyed the lessons—I because of my disappointment over Mrs. Jackson, and Danny because he hated the piano, he said—but both of us loved to ride away with our father.

Danny sat in the front. My parents always spoke of him as energetic. I was a calmer child and could be trusted to sit alone in the back seat and keep out of trouble. I loved my brother so I collaborated with my father in this way. I never took it as a slight. Under Dad's watch, Danny behaved himself all the way to our lessons and home again. He chattered without stopping, it seemed, but I knew that my father was soothing, correcting, and guiding him. Danny was his only son.

In the back, I was thinking. I'd become aware of myself, around this time, as a person who thought. Thinking gave my head a sense of fullness, of contentment, like my stomach after supper or my skin after a bath. I felt that my thoughts were interesting, even profound. They seemed to form a continuous, pleasant motion that originated in me. I stared at my father's neck and thought of ropes or columns or trees. I saw his ears, tight to his skull, with their golden ridges, and thought about things shaped oddly, and his hair cut close at the back and sides and longer on the top with its crisp blond wave, and thought of hills, steep on one side and gradual on the other. Of the rolling hills of Alberta where we lived, which we wound over and around, driving to our lessons. I thought about hills in general, and what they might signify. I tried to think through the fact that the man seated in front of me with his specific parts, which made a whole, was the man who was also my father. To think through the fact that I came from him and from my mother, at that moment making supper at home. I wasn't thinking about the act of sex, which was vague to me then, so much as the fact of my existence. Because of his, because of hers.

Danny took his piano lesson first. Mrs. Jackson prodded while he poked, and both soon tired of their mutual obligations. When it was my turn, I felt I had to mollify the keys, to comfort them because of my stubborn, disinterested brother.

He didn't last with the lessons beyond that year; my parents let him quit. But he learned one thing, and that was "Chopsticks." Not from Mrs. Jackson but from me, and I'd picked it up from my best friend Betty, who got it from her older sister Anne. Danny and I must have played that silly thing a thousand times. His part was the c and g chords in the bass, repeated in triplets, and mine the two-handed dancing sticks of sound high above them, notes that chased each other up and down, meeting and parting and meeting again. Danny yelled "Faster!" after every round and we increased our speed until we or the song fell apart, both of us laughing hysterically.

I'm hearing "Chopsticks" now, two girls who look to be the ages Danny and I were that year, pounding it out on the upright in the lounge of the seniors' home. They get through it twice before a nurse manages, out of breath, to rush in and shush them.

"No, no, no," she says. "It's much too loud for the old people." She casts a scolding look at the girls' mother.

Most of the elderly people in the room are hard of hearing or even deaf; "Chopsticks" probably hurts my ears and hers the most. Some of the seniors, in fact, raised their lax heads with interest while the girls squealed and played. My father turned toward the racket as well.

I press my hand over his. "Hey Dad, remember that? Chopsticks? Danny and me?"

My father swivels his head to my voice and gazes at me with an expression of cool assessment that might be compelling on the face of a younger man but on his face expresses dementia. It's impossible to know by now what he perceives, what's happening in his head. Whether he wonders who's sitting beside him, and why she uses words like *Dad*, and *chopsticks*, and *Danny*.

The girls, who are wearing identical pink shorts and white T-shirts, flounce onto empty chairs beside their mother. She's visiting her aunt, talking a stream of homey news and gossip while the other woman nods. The aunt's hair looks tissue-soft and freshly curled; it must have been her day at the facility's hairdresser. She radiates sweetness but there's no more recognition in her face than in my father's. She nods, nod after nod, like a music box unwinding the single melody it's been programmed to play.

My father's head sinks back to its half-lowered position where he has a view of his brown polyester pants and the flaccid blue-veined hands on his lap.

In May, the week of Danny's eleventh birthday, my father came into my room where I was reading *Little Women* and sat down on the edge of the bed. He asked me how I liked the book.

I said I liked it very much.

He asked who my favourite character was and I said, "Jo."

"That's what I've heard," he said. "All the girls like Jo."

Then he said, "Well, my Jo-Jo Patty, it's Danny's birthday tomorrow and I've planned a surprise for him. I've arranged for the two of you to ride home on the train. I'll have to bring the car home, of course.

"Danny's crazy for trains," he continued. "As you know."

"I know he is, Daddy," I said. Whenever we spotted the train on our way home from our lessons, Danny launched into pleading: to catch up, to pass, to go faster.

If our father obliged, the car filled with a torrent of noise— our own accelerating engine, the train's roar and clatter beside us, my brother's yipping glee directed to the trainmen who waved. As if he thought they could hear him over the tremor of metal on metal.

My father asked me to keep the train ride a secret, and to keep an eye on Danny during our little adventure. He said, "I know it's not *your* birthday, Patty, but I think you'll find it special too."

I suppose I was still inside the cadences of *Little Women,* so I leapt forward and flung my arms about his neck. I said it would be wonderful. I said, "Thank you, Daddy, thank you very very much."

My father squeezed me back, kissed my ear, and said, "You're very very welcome."

The train Danny and I boarded the next day travelled up the spur line twice a week, carrying freight. Most people got around by car by then, but half a wagon was outfitted with seats, just in case. The seats gave off a prim air of humiliation, on account of people not using them much, I supposed. They were brown and stiff and plain. They seemed dusty, not luxurious as I'd hoped. But Danny was excited and I consoled myself that it was our first trip and there were sure to be more trips, on other kinds of trains.

I was also disappointed that we were not alone. A young man

slouched in the corner seat, four rows back. He was wearing glasses and a flat cap. His face and demeanour seemed flat as well but I may have imagined this later, as the look of stupidity, or cunning perhaps.

We perched in the front, Danny by the window. The train pulled out of town and there, driving on the road beside us, was our father in our Chevrolet. Danny waved and shouted. Now it was Dad who couldn't hear him yell, and we who felt the whirring clank of the train wheels, the click of the rails under our feet. Our father seemed small and rigid at a distance, like a different person, as if he'd changed with the strain of keeping up with us.

The train whistle sounded at a crossing. Something was pressing against my chest. My eyes darted downward. A pinkish hand with fat spread fingers straddled my blouse. The middle finger was curved and its tip rested on one of my buttons.

The hand was grotesque, like an insect. What did it want? It pushed me against the seatback, pushed against my heart, now drumming madly in panic and confusion. It paralyzed me.

Danny must have noticed something and he reeled round.

He said, "Whaddya think you're doing?" It came out high-pitched, more animated than annoyed, as if he and a buddy were scrapping over a pencil or marble, over some minor possession.

But then he twisted further, half rose, and his voice gained solid edge. "You! You leave my sister alone!"

The hand lifted, the arm withdrew. Its withdrawal was graceful, almost elegant, as if, in fact, there'd been no pressure within it at all. Footsteps I'd not heard coming now moved briskly away and Danny and I turned back to the window. My brother resumed his boisterous commentary but I couldn't speak. The sensation of the hand still vibrated on my chest. Nothing showed on my blouse but I felt its residue like a smudge. I wanted the train ride to be over.

Arriving at the depot in our town, we saw Dad on the

platform, and Mom and our younger sisters waiting with him as well, and my throat clenched with joy and relief. It seemed as if we'd been separated for days.

"Hey, son!" my father shouted as we stepped off the train. "How was *that*?"

"Great ride!" Danny said. He swaggered. "And I took care of Patty too!"

My parents chuckled and my father winked at me, as if to say that he knew very well who had taken care of whom.

The girls and their mother are saying goodbye to the sweet, nodding aunt. The sisters tussle and giggle and then they rush to the piano. They pound out "Chopsticks" again, a race against the return of the disapproving nurse. Once, twice, and they dash out the door after their mother. The room seems empty without them.

Sometimes I wonder why I come.

We know *them*, even if they don't know *us*, my peers and I say, when we discuss our aging parents. We offer each other encouragements like this about their decline, their depressions, their lingering departures. About their Alzheimer's, heart attacks, strokes, and diseases. You have to die of something, we say. Not lies exactly, these sentences, but a litany insufficient for what we are feeling when we visit and despair of them. What we're trying to say is how sad that they leave; how sad that they don't; how sad that in leaving they leave so little behind, not even crumbs like Hansel and Gretel left to guide our way back to them. We speak as if their deaths concern us more than they matter to them.

But I have no idea what we might say that would get at the truth of our losses.

I wish that I'd told my father, a teacher of social studies and literature all his working life, that I was the one who understood trains the way he did, not as iron, wind, and noise but as technology gathering myth, weaving through history like the mane of smoke a steam engine tosses behind its back, running beside us and then away across the vast fields of the world. That mournful horn-song in its wake. All those station farewells and arrivals. All that dreaming in a dark cocoon while the landscape disappears. How you might read a book and discover years later you remembered nothing of its contents but could still recall with astonishing vividness the experience of reading it on a train, from city A to city B. How the train carries you away through empty countryside that seems to be waiting, just for you.

And Dad and I knew the dangers.

I never told him what the two of us had had in common. It's because everything about trains seemed—for so many years—to belong to him and Danny especially, and then that connection was broken when Danny tried to beat the evening transport sweeping down the tracks just east of Regina, he and his orange Thunderbird crushed and tossed aside as if they were flim-flam in the business of traversing the prairies.

My parents and sisters and I liked to tell ourselves he missed us so much he forgot to be careful at the crossing. But Danny only knew speed. "Faster, faster" was his cry.

I realize now that his calling was equal to mine. He dreamed of becoming a pilot. Maybe an astronaut, he said.

"You'll have to put your nose to the grindstone then," our father would say. "Pilots need to know a thing or two."

And finally, Danny started to study. My parents said he'd smartened up. They were jubilant when he went to university.

I sit beside my father once a week. Sometimes I talk, just in case. Sometimes I'm tempted to play one of the classical pieces he loved, pieces I now teach and perform. But the piano in the lounge is out of tune and I just can't bring myself to do it.

It's sunny in the corner where I wheel him in his chair. I like the gentle fall of light over his now-bent neck, over his transparent scalp and the clotted strands of his hair. Perhaps we collaborate again. He's still here and so I remember: my younger dad, my brother Danny, music that stirs and aches, how awareness grows, how I believed I'd been summoned to think.

My thoughts swell, and they seem profound.

An Advance on an Uncertain Future

Thom knows the way to Grand Forks, but he unfolded the map in the car before he left; he double-checked. He traced the #75 out of Winnipeg with his finger. A highway like a leg, he thought, like the long leg of a dancer, knee bent at Morris, toes dug into Emerson as if to give the border the boot, scatter some loose Dakota dirt over the prairies. And the #29 below it, dangling to their destination.

They're sliding down the lovely leg, he and Angie, sliding easily now in the pearl blue Echo over the flat plain of southern Manitoba, through the vast pale light of an April afternoon, the landscape winter-drab, but surely—he believes—cracking under the surface, swelling with thaw. Stirring. The car he shares with his sisters, which he claimed for today, is riding well.

He's watching the road but his sense of Angie beside him— her round expressive face, long black curls, arched brows, and brown eyes—overlaps with his attention to driving, as if she's perched behind his glasses. The sense of her bright red jacket and matching knitted hat over the tumble of her hair; the sense

13

of her shoulder solid and near, and how their shoulders would match if they put them together.

Thom's mood is optimistic, even extravagant, Angie beside him, and the two of them heading for the States. It's election year and their southern neighbour seems closer than ever, all the news and talk about the Democratic nomination, and contenders Hillary Clinton and Barack Obama coming, both of them, to the rally in North Dakota. He and Angie will be there, and it elevates Grand Forks in his mind to a city where spring has arrived. A city like a field already plowed. He's thinking of this trip as their first date. He hopes Angie will call it that too.

His major is history; hers is literature. They met in rhetoric class, where they landed in the same work group and five times wandered amiably to the cafeteria together after class. Both had picked up their professor's enthusiasm for American politics. Their professor insisted his students listen to speeches on television or the web. He often cited Senators Clinton and Obama as examples of certain points he was trying to make. He said the Democratic primary in this year's election was turning out to be a drama of historic proportions. He mentioned the North Dakota rally.

"It's a double feature," Thom told Angie when he finally got up his nerve—just this morning—to tell her he'd decided to go. Would she want to come too? He explained, in case she'd forgotten, that both candidates would be there. Unusual, he reminded her, for a sparsely populated, Republican state.

Angie had laughed and said, "Of course I want to come. It sounds like way more fun than finishing papers or studying for exams." She told him she would cut her afternoon class and hurry home to get her things.

It's too early to speak of their encounters in rhetoric class as if they mean something that adheres to them as a pair, but in the car they build from them. They repeat the things they've read and heard in the course. They repeat some of the observations they shared while walking to the cafeteria.

"Something's definitely shifting," Thom says. "It may be significant."

Thom rarely speaks up in class but so far, heading south down the highway, he's doing most of the talking. "Worldwide, I mean," he says. "And our country, of course, adjunct to all that. Odd that we should care, I suppose. It's not our country. Not our election."

"Totally. I know what you mean."

"Not that I don't like Canada." Thom says this firmly, as if to establish the coordinates of a mathematics problem. "But America's got the power. Now, I mean. So I feel like we're in on it too … I'd like to be, at least."

"Yeah," she says. "I know what you mean."

He tips his head back against the headrest. He's ready to move on to something original. "My dad's always reminiscing," he says. "If there's anything in the news connected to the sixties and that. He'll say what he was doing when Kennedy was killed. And Martin Luther King. He tells me about Vietnam or Watergate as if I've never heard of them. Tells me how Dylan or the Beatles arrived on the scene. Memories about stuff we're still aware of, listening to."

"I have the Beatles commemorative set," Angie offers. Shyly, like she's sharing a secret.

Thom glances at her and she turns her head and their eyes meet. "Hey!" he says. "That's great."

They're silent for a kilometre or so, perhaps in honour of the Beatles, and then Thom picks up the conversation again, saying he didn't mean to give the wrong impression about him and his dad. They get along great. They're close. But it's hard in a way, his parents and so much stuff they remember.

One reason he wants to be at the rally, he continues, is that if Obama gets to be the Democratic nominee, and then gets to be president, it will be something for him. For him and for her, he says; for their generation. A marker. A memory for them in particular.

"Do you know what I mean?" he asks.

"Totally," she says.

"It doesn't seem weird?"

"Not at all." Then, "Hillary's historic too. A double feature, like you said this morning."

Thom murmurs agreement but wonders if he should emphasize he's hoping for Obama. He thinks Angie is too, but maybe there's a feeling of loyalty, one female to another, he's unaware of. Such loyalty wouldn't be automatic for his mother and sisters, he thinks, but does his knowledge of the women in his family apply to Angie?

The road curves widely, then straightens, and Thom remembers someone in his first-year psychology course saying that men wear their vehicles like skin, and how it angered him because he felt it wasn't true; not true of him at least, for he'd never belonged to the high school strata of boys who cared about speed or motor size or the sound of a muffler. But after that, the Echo, coloured "aqua ice opalescent," which his sisters called cute, embarrassed him, like a flare-up of his acne. But it seems bigger now, this reliable car, small and strong and responsive to the road and to his yearnings for Angie. To the significance of this day.

"I guess we have 9/11," he says. "Our generation, I mean. The footage of that plane going into that tower. It's like, iconic."

"Yeah. I know what you mean."

"My parents are cynical about the Bushes and everything," he says. "They like Obama too."

"My folks don't talk politics or history much," Angie says. "Though Mom did mention that Hillary's been through a lot—with that *Bill*."

They laugh.

"My dad's a Bill too," she explains. "And my folks are divorced."

Thom shifts his hands on the steering wheel, widens his grip. "I'm sorry," he says.

"No, no. It's okay. It's a long time ago."

Thom is suddenly apprehensive. "Is it boring you, all this talk of politics, as if we're still in class or something?"

"No, not at all!" Her voice is fervent and he believes her.

Angie feels the car's coziness and the hum of their progress as a kind of sling that contains and compresses her. She worries she's too heavy, that she'll be fat someday. She's big-boned, like her father, whom her mother divorced. She thinks Thom hasn't noticed yet. He seems old-fashioned. Not that she minds, she thinks, if it means that he likes her the way she is. She wonders if she should tell him about her mother's multiple sclerosis, how they just found out, how they're hoping for the best and that she said, last week, "Jeepers, if Hillary can run for president, I can fight back this crazy disease." Her mother says "Jeepers" a lot.

Thom's words break her thoughts. "But do you ever find yourself afraid?" he asks. "Kennedy gone early, and Martin Luther King. I mean, if there's another assassination or something... Sometimes I have worries I've never mentioned aloud."

"Go ahead," she says.

He sighs. "That some radical Islamic coalition will conquer the world in our time. Reverse the Battle of Vienna. Or China takes over. It's not that long, you know, relatively speaking, that America has been first nation of the earth. China has the people, the money, the motivation. To make our history miserable with unfamiliar laws and languages. Payback."

Angie doesn't answer immediately. He's finished but she's still listening to what he said.

Then she says, "You're right. It makes sense for you to worry. You're a history major. You know how things can go."

He chuckles, but she hears the lack of conviction in his response, and it comforts her. She's glad he understands that she didn't mean her comment as a joke.

Thom's fears have been real but in speaking them aloud to Angie they've turned into something that sounds like a report, as if they happened a long time ago and all their circumstances have been forgiven. Turned into history and proven false. And now they've disappeared—how strange they seemed, made audible, revealed and tamed just like that!—and he's pleased. He finds himself forming sentences for the future, hears himself reciting them as if to his children. *We witnessed the u.s. put a black man in the White House. Imagine that, after their long and racist history... And did you know we went to see that black man, that President Obama, speaking at a great rally in North Dakota?*

Thom knows he's lunging to speculation, wildly, but his hope is as sure as a rope and he's hand over hand on it. He's telling the little creatures, all ears, these wonderful words. *Your mother and I drove down to Grand Forks one afternoon in 2008. It was the year we met. We heard him speak. He promised things could change. It was only the beginning for the two of us too, and that's how you've come to be...*

He sees the children clapping their hands and squealing with delight.

When they pass St. Jean Baptiste there's a lull in their talking which may become awkward unless one of them thinks of something to say. Thom mutters, "Soup pea capital of Manitoba," meaning the town, but Angie asks, "Are you hungry?" She rummages through her quilted homemade bag. "I brought us a snack."

She lifts out two plastic cases and pops their lids. She hands one to Thom. "Trail mix," she says.

Thom says, "Great! Thanks!" He sets the container between his legs.

"Healthy," she says, "though there's Smarties in it too. I have a weakness for Smarties."

She regrets this immediately. What if he's thinking, whoa girl, not Smarties, not for you, just when she's feeling fine with him? Thinner.

But there's something else. A doubt, a shard of anxiety hurting like a sliver does, and her hand reacting, touching every object in her bag, one after the other: makeup case, notebook, pen, brush, book she needs to finish for her Canadian literature class, taming gel, pink iPod in its case.

She flips through each item again, in the opposite order. iPod, gel, book, brush...

While her fingers take inventory as if by Braille, Angie's inner eye is clear. It sweeps the rooms at home and what she sees becomes even clearer, zoomed in to her, enlarged: her wallet and passport lying on her dresser. Lying in front of the clutter she pushed back to set them there, the passport because she retrieved it from the filing box where her family keeps important documents and the wallet because she checked her money, had none, so raided her mother's grocery envelope. There, the wallet and the passport on the corner of the dresser; ready. She made the snack (recalling how he'd munched on trail mix during some of their group work, and wanting to surprise him), threw the containers into her bag, ran to get her jacket.

Everything was such a rush. Thom had asked her only this morning. He told her the time he would be by for her, and then he reminded her, in a teasing tone, that he was always on time. Because she was often late.

But she didn't keep him waiting.

The passport and the wallet are not in her bag but on the dresser. Angie imagines them clinging together reproachfully, self-consciously, as if displayed behind museum glass. Her fingers page through the contents of her bag once more, but it's mere idleness now.

"You won't believe it," she says.

"What?"

"I left my passport at home on the dresser where I put it with my wallet when I went to get the snack and oh, it's unbelievable!" Her dilemma and disbelief emerge in a single breath.

She said he wouldn't believe it and it seems to be true; he's not reacting.

But after a moment he asks, "They're still taking driver's licences, aren't they? I don't think they're requiring passports yet, are they?"

"I left my wallet too." The last word high; a wail.

Thom is remembering how disorganized Angie has been in their rhetoric work group, in spite of getting the top marks in the class.

Angie is wondering why Thom hadn't reminded her. Isn't he the guy who claims he's so far ahead of the organizational curve that he's already come back to a handwritten list on paper? Always a bright yellow rectangle at the top of his daily pile, like a lemon he grabs every morning to suck on all day.

But neither utters recriminations. It's a gentle salvage operation they're involved in now. Each lifts intermittent, polite fingerfuls of nuts, raisins, seeds, and candy to their mouths and while one talks, the other crunches and chews.

Thom says, "Why don't we try at the border anyway, tell the officers, see what happens?"

"No," she says. "No. It won't work. It'll be a hassle and then you'll have to turn around." She doesn't want to say that minus wallet and passport she feels conspicuous. Larger and darker. Her mother is a cross-border shopper so Angie knows the rigidities, the variable humours, of customs officials. They intimidate her and she'll be nervous, and then she'll act nervous, she'll look suspicious, and next thing she knows, they'll be searching for drugs.

Thom says they should forget about the rally then. He sounds stricken.

Or, his voice jumping back brightly, could they turn back for it? Or, is there someone who could bring them her passport if they stopped and waited?

"No. No. No." Angie's voice is quiet. Adamant. There isn't enough time to return to Winnipeg and set out again. And there's no one home at her house.

She'll find some place in Emerson to wait, she says. There has to be *some* place. He *has* to go.

"I have my book"—her own bright suggestion, as if she's planned it all along. "*Surfacing*. I'm late for my last CanLit report, though I got an extension. I'll finish the book and write the report, that's what I'll do. Later, you'll tell me all about the rally."

She persuades him, too easily, she thinks. But she's the one who forgot her passport, so what should she expect?

At Emerson, the border town, they turn in at a small building with the word EAT on the roof. The young woman at the counter says yes, certainly, Angie can sit here the evening if she likes. She beams smiles of encouragement and understanding.

Thom gives Angie a twenty for supper.

"I'll pay you back," she says.

"We'll argue over it later."

"We weren't arguing, Thom, were we?" Angie feels afraid.

"I didn't mean it like that. You have to have supper." Thom wishes he could kiss Angie goodbye, arm around her waist, lift her off her feet the way soldiers bid farewell to their girls on train station platforms in the last world war. He knows the photos from history books. Kisses as an advance on an uncertain future.

"Don't get into trouble now," he says instead, lightly. "You don't have ID."

They laugh at that, and she says, "See you later, Thom, and have fun. I'm feeling really silly about this. Honestly, I could kick myself."

"Stuff happens," he says.

Angie sits in a booth with a red-topped table, on a bench wrapped in cheap red leather, elbows up, chin in her hands, hair tickling her wrists. She's in a funk, and her funk is biding its time.

She told Thom her parents never talked about culture or politics, as if they'd managed to bypass the overweening arc of memory belonging to their peers, but now she remembers her mother saying, "I'm no feminist, but you girls nowadays take everything for granted. You have no idea how it used to be, not even all that very long ago. Remember Billie Jean King?"

Angie had blurted "Who?" but then she'd realized her mother was asking Angie's stepfather and he said, "Don't remind me."

I'm a lot like Barack Obama, she thinks, my family strange, my identity in fragments. I can't say where I fit.

But she makes the best of things. Sometimes, out of the blue, her mother will say, "Angie's amazing."

Well, she's never been a talker but then she'll get an insight, something new and true and it builds up inside her as if it's inevitable, and then she jumps into things, into a class discussion, for example, intensely, like a fireworks display. Once launched, she has to continue, startling even herself at the flower-burst of her words, the way their logic and language dazzle in the atmosphere after she's finished and her speech fades away. This quality of hers draws attention. Thom's eyes widened that first time in rhetoric class and then he smiled at her. As far as she's concerned, that's when it started between them.

He's the policy wonk, his mouth prim and precise, like the New York senator's, even when he rambles.

And she's his flame of hope.

But, stupid her, she left her passport behind. So she'll read the stupid book, write the stupid overdue paper.

She orders a burger. Before she pays for it, Angie presses Thom's twenty bill hard against her lips.

There are cars waiting behind him at the crossing. He can't take the time to tell the story, to ask about the chances of Angie— back in that Emerson café—getting in. He'd go back if it were possible, he thinks, but the officer seems impatient. He's probably Republican.

Once through, once on the North Dakota highway south, Thom tries to tamp down his huge disappointment. He turns on the radio, lands on a station with country music and ads for farm implements and weed control. The ads and the music annoy him—he feels snobbish, and it's a feeling tight and bitter—but they distract him too. He doesn't move the dial.

When he merges into the noisy, weaving column of people gathered outside the Alerus Center, Thom's enthusiasm for the rally finally returns. He spots some Winnipeggers he knows, including Steve from his rhetoric class, who waves for him to move up closer, join his group.

Steve asks Thom if he came alone.

"I got as far as Emerson with Angie.—Angie Pauls."

"Angie!" Steve's admiration is obvious and a balm to Thom's half-deserted fantasies, to the impossibility now of *In Grand Forks, that evening in April, your mother and I...*

"She forgot her passport and wallet."

"I guess I'm not surprised," Steve says. He grins. Thom grins too. He says "Yeah," though he wants to protect Angie from both of them and their offhand critique.

He took too long, gathering the courage to invite her to come. No wonder she forgot. He should have asked, "Passport, camera? You, me, are we and ours all here?" A little game: check check check. He should never make assumptions.

The arena doors open and everyone surges in, seeks seats, a good view. The Center is packed. Thom overhears someone saying it can hold more than twenty thousand people. The gathering is loud and he and Steve and his friends are jumpy, as if they have the jitters, though it's only excitement, and he's relieved that the emotion seems as real to him in the arena as in the rallies he's seen on television, that it's not letting him down, not this rally at least, especially as the evening reaches its peak: the man he has come to see and experience, that resonant voice, the repeats and pauses, the ends of sentences hanging in the air like kites in the wind.

"We know this election is our chance to start over, to finally come together and solve the problems we've been talking about for generations!" Senator Obama cries out to them. "To put America on a different path! And that's why I'm running"—the cheers increase—"for President of the United States of America."

Thom claps, whistles, stomps his feet, shouts along. "Yes—We—Can! Yes—We—Can!" The tall man's easy stride, his gestures, his words create a kind of breeze. Thom sways in it, along with everyone else. He's hopeful for this man, and he's happy.

It's been nearly an hour since Obama finished and Hillary Clinton hasn't appeared.

"I'm leaving," Thom tells Steve. "Angie will be waiting."

"Gotcha. Angie over Hillary. No contest there. I wouldn't mind leaving myself."

Thom ignores the hint to invite Steve to ride back with him.

Going north, traffic is light. The miles pass slowly in the purple dusk. Thom notices nothing but the road, one overpass crossing the highway after another, the car all strain and exertion now, and the way back narrower than before, like an endless tunnel of shadow and reflection.

His faults form a list in his mind. Leaving Angie. Agreeing with Steve. Not thinking of her once during the senator's speech.

He wonders if he talked too much earlier, while they were side by side. He sorts through the layers of their conversation, scans them, tries to remember how she responded. She was consistently friendly, nodding and murmuring her interest. He remembers the scent that lifted from her body like a wisp of smoke when they stopped in Emerson and she shifted and loosened her seat belt. Something sweet and citrus-like.

But she didn't seem to mind missing the rally. Was she glad to be rid of him? Did she think him a worrier, all that talk about the world possibly ruined in their generation? Their turn to be oppressed? Was she thinking, enough of your gloom already?

He still wants her. And it wasn't gloom, he'd say if he had the chance to repeat it. It was unburdening.

He also knows he hasn't forgiven her for forgetting her wallet and passport.

At the border, the Canadian customs officer is curious about the rally in Grand Forks. Thom says he left early. He doesn't add anything else. He fears the drive to Winnipeg will be strenuous, like a long climb up a ladder, and it makes him tired to think of it.

And here he is now, at the first rung. In the warm orange light of the restaurant window he sees Angie's dark head, bowed, beautiful as a halo. She's taken off the red hat and her jacket. She's wearing black. She's reading or writing. He knows she'll write one draft, or two at the most, and she'll get an A on it. But did she bring paper? Is she writing on the serviettes?

Thom turns off the motor. He bends out of his small blue car to get her.

The Rocking Chair

Old George Martens liked to say, "When my time is up, I'm taking nothing along."

His children tired of hearing it. Of course he wouldn't, they thought. But they'd been taught respect, so they let it be, let the pronouncement hang in the air as if original and not a cliché. As if it needed further contemplation.

Which it did when he died, suddenly, at eighty-eight. Then they remembered how often he'd said it, how vividly true it had turned out to be, for he hadn't taken his body, discovered by Norma, his bed, his navy flannel pajamas, or the flowered quilt lying over him rumpled that he'd once shared with his wife. Not the underlined Bible, alarm clock, or anything else.

And soon they knew, also, how little he'd left behind: the tiny apartment's worth of personal effects, and less than six thousand dollars in the bank. Compared to what he and his thrifty Maria had managed to snug down for retirement, this was pathetic. Had she—their mother—been alive, she would have staunched the flow of the account. But she'd died ten years earlier and in the decade since, their father had been giving their savings away, one donation after the other to every church or charity that asked for his help. It seemed he'd forgotten how frugal she'd been.

Or maybe he remembered too well. In the memo line of every cheque, in his neatest, wavering hand, George Martens had printed "In memory of my beloved Maria."

Leonard, the youngest, was an accountant. Every year, he'd helped his father with his annual tax return and every year he reported to his brother Harold and his sister Norma that he'd urged their father to leave the principal intact, to generate income he would need if things got worse and he'd have to move to the other side, meaning the acute care wing where expenses were higher. But the older man would say, "I get money from the government. I'm sure there'll be enough to see me through." He always added, "I'm sure the Lord will provide."

Leonard admitted to his siblings that he was frustrated by his father's attitude. And shamed by it too.

"He's a good man," Norma reminded her brothers in these conversations. She looked in on their father nearly every day, saw the mail coming in, going out. "He's helping a lot of other people."

The brothers recognized the disappointment in her voice and Harold would say, "His mind is clear. And isn't it something—his generosity?"·

They had to agree. "None of us really needs it," Leonard said.

The mild shock of their father's death and the details of making arrangements drew the three of them closer. They were all in their fifties but his passing had rendered them orphans—Norma used the word—and they felt freed and young again. Didn't the deceased matter mainly to the three of them? Their own spouses and children seemed milestones they'd passed in a brief ambitious dash away from their childhoods, a kind of detour now from what was essential: their growing up together in the pale blue bungalow on McKay. And memories like their father bursting through the back door, shouting, "What's up with everyone? I've got a surprise!"

Once it was a puppy, once a new ball and bat, and another time—almost unbelievable because of his views on "worldly" entertainment—tickets to the circus.

They didn't speak now of the last low figure on their late father's bank account—their three-way inheritance—though Harold ventured that it was certainly a blessing their father had prepaid his funeral, and Leonard and Norma murmured that this was a blessing indeed. Each understood; and each was glad to have the others.

Their father's rooms at the seniors' highrise had to be emptied before the end of the month. Norma knew there was nothing of value left. They'd divided the lace tablecloths and china after their mother's death, and their father had lived sparsely. She could have done it herself. But she wasn't ready to leave their resurrected, golden past. When a burst of rain is unexpected, strangers rush to the nearest shelter and may find themselves sharing an adventure, and so it was for Norma with her brothers. She said they should dispose of their father's belongings together.

"All of us," she repeated, "need to be there."

She was delayed the afternoon they'd arranged to meet. Harold and Leonard let themselves into the apartment but they weren't sure how to begin without their sister's direction. The place smelled sour.

Harold switched on the air conditioning. "Is she bringing boxes?" he asked.

Leonard said he had no idea.

"I'd say box the works and take it to the secondhand."

"Sounds good to me," Leonard said. "I've got the pickup. I'll just take my chair and deliver the rest."

Harold was studying the titles of his father's one-shelf library. "Chair?" He straightened. "I'm taking the rocking chair."

Leonard straightened too, in order to ease his hands into his pockets. "Dad told me I could have the rocking chair."

Both had immediately concealed their surprise at the other's claim. Both took a small step forward.

"Sorry," Harold said. "Dad offered it to me. More than once. Just last month, in fact, we were talking and he said, Take the chair, Harold, after I go. I want you to have it."

Leonard's response came in a rush. "But Dad and I made it together. He told me it was practically mine, I did so much of the work. He said he'd just use it until he died."

"It's nothing special as far as chairs go."

"Well, whatever." Leonard's voice rose a tone. "I know the work that it was, to make it."

"Sorry, Leonard, but he gave it to me. I'd come in and he'd be sitting there, reading his Bible or listening to the broadcasts, you know, and he said, Harold, it's been an answer to prayer, you in the ministry, and I'd say, this is the picture I'll always remember, Dad, of you, sitting there in your rocking chair, doing what you can—and he said, Take the chair when I'm gone to remember your father and—"

"He gave it to *me*."

Harold heard the petulance in his brother's voice, vibrating slightly like neon. He saw the sarcastic set of his mouth. "What a windy talker!" he remembered Leonard throwing at him when they were boys, when he'd wanted to hurt him. "You'll be a preacher, I suppose!"

He remembered lobbing it back. "What a baby, Leonard,

always getting your way, everyone falling for your charm and your tricks and no idea what you're up to!"

And once he'd yelled, just before slamming the door, "And yes, maybe I *will* be a preacher!"

And now he was.

The apartment was on the seventh floor. Harold stepped to the window and peered down, looking for Norma's car in the parking lot. The car roofs gleamed like mirrors under the sun and he couldn't distinguish one from the other.

He was about to remark on the heat when he remembered that he and Leonard weren't exactly friendly at the moment so he kept quiet instead and let his mind wander over the view, the trees and houses in the distance, the broad cheerful spread of summer green. He liked the peace of it. He preferred happy endings and now he was hearing the story unwinding again, the story he'd told in his sermon several Sundays ago, the last before his father's death.

This week I visited my father and there he was, eighty-eight but still bright as a whistle and smiling, good teeth for a man his age, doing what he's always doing when I come. Rocking, maybe reading, maybe listening to the radio or one of his cassettes, his mind at attention. When he moved over from the house we asked him, How about a brand new chair? The place is small, but there's room for a chair. One that reclines at the press of a button, or maybe tips you forward and helps you onto your feet again. And he said, Don't you know how comfortable my old rocking chair still is? That Mother made the cushion, and this was her final afghan? It's perfectly suitable. Sturdy and soft enough. Everything I need in a chair. Like my faith, he said. Everything I need. And true.

Harold heard himself telling the story, felt the eyes of his parishioners as one upon him, their listening offered back to him as palpable as sound. The listening that sustained him, people eager for his words as if they were touch. Scattered chuckles like sparkles in the air at the little joke about new-fangled recliners.

They called him Pastor Harry. They'd given him a vote of affirmation in the spring. It was because of his preaching, he thought, and because of what he'd learned over the years. More than anything else, he'd learned, people want to be noticed. So he'd honed the art of noticing them. Reaching out a hand to greet, using first names. And he spent effort on his sermons, writing them out and practising until they sounded informal and uncomposed, as if they'd come to him in the course of conversation. As if he was speaking to only one of them. Each, and only one.

Now he heard Leonard clearing his throat. It seemed an accusation, not of their sister Norma, who was late, but of him, daydreaming about a sermon he'd delivered. As if his brother had heard the story and was completely unimpressed. As if he wondered what point it was trying to make.

He'd been trying to make the point that faith like his father's, though ancient, was still reliable. Still good enough.

His visits to his father had usually been short. His work as pastor kept him very busy. Once a week, he'd hurried in, hurried out. But he'd responded with patience to his father's regular question, "Are souls being saved?" He never told him he didn't use those words anymore. And he'd always taken a compliment away with him. "Wonderful to have a son in the church," George Martens might say. Or, "You're doing well and I'm proud of you."

I'm proud of you. Harold wanted his father's chair.

He turned to face the room. "Under the law," he said, "it's the last directions that hold."

Leonard lowered himself onto the bed. "There's nothing in the will," he said. "And verbally... How do I know that you're telling the truth?"

Harold seethed. "Oh come on!" he said. "Neither of us is a liar."

Leonard replied, too calmly, that one of them certainly excelled at exaggeration.

Harold swivelled to the window again, hoping the waves of tension in his body would subside. He and Leonard hadn't argued this way since they'd left home in their late teens. It surprised him how quickly the aggravation returned, as fast and beguiling as an unbroken habit.

"This is the first time I've heard you say the chair is yours," Harold said after some time. He spoke toward the window and his voice was even. "Dad never referred to it that way."

"I made the thing with him!" Leonard exclaimed. "He said it would be mine!

"A few hours. How many years ago was that?"

Leonard leapt up from the bed where he was sitting, and the sound of it startled Harold into a half turn.

"You're not the only one who was close to Dad!" Leonard hissed. "Just because you're a preacher!"

Three steps and Leonard had reached the washroom. He coughed; he spit into the sink. He had very nearly added, "Thank goodness Linda and I changed neighbourhoods and had an excuse to change churches, so I don't have to listen to your sermons any more."

He nearly said it.

It wasn't what he wanted to say. Not at all. He wanted to explain the chair.

It's a comb-back Windsor. I found the pattern in a magazine. The seat is ash. The comb is elm. I turned the leg, the stumps for the arms. He wanted bulges and valleys, something ornate. I said, let's keep it simple. I talked him into this pattern. We went through every step. We did it together. Every day I was over at their place. I'd thought to make it for Linda. Then she changed her mind and said she didn't want a rocking chair. Meanwhile, Dad and I were testing it. He claimed it'd be for Mom, but he never had her sit down on it. We made it for him. And for me. We're the same size. I drilled and shaped the arms. Joined the arms and uprights. Assembled the underframe, the upper components. Fitted the rockers. Chiselled, shaped, and hollowed the seat. They're not upper-class kind of chairs but we made it elegant anyway. We didn't talk much but I was happy. You're good with your hands, Dad told me, you're better at this than I am. He said that, even though he was the carpenter and I'd become an accountant.

Leonard emerged from the bathroom. "They used to be called digestive chairs," he said. "Did you know that?—Did you know that Dad had excellent digestion?"

Harold gaped at Leonard as if he'd asked him a riddle. But he felt composed again and was pleased about that so he asked Leonard, casually as if discussing the weather, whether he had problems with digestion; is that why he wanted the chair?

Then, not waiting for an answer, Harold said, "This time, Leonard, I'm sticking to my guns. You think I'll give in, as always, but I won't."

"As *always*?"

Norma rushed through the door at this precise and fortunate moment. She started explaining why she was late, then stopped as if sniffing the air.

She said, "What's the matter now?"

Nothing had been the matter for years, but she pressed upon the *now* as if they'd just been squabbling over the comics in Saturday's paper or their after-school chores.

The scent of tension hung in the air. Norma believed it a deficiency peculiar to males that they couldn't manage conflict.

They let it cook too long, she said, and bottled it up, and then the bottle broke and made such a terrible mess. She'd studied mediation in her management training. She felt she had a natural bent in a peaceful direction. She was willing to own her strengths, she said.

Norma's husband Kevin once grumbled that if she'd been around, Cain and Abel would have had to talk things through. Ditto Jacob and Esau, and the McCain brothers over in the Maritimes.

She'd taken this as a compliment and added a biblical example of her own. "And the Sons of Thunder might have been the Sunshine Boys," she laughed.

Now Harold told Norma that the matter was the rocking chair. He ambled to a new position in the room, against the kitchenette stove.

Norma squinted at the chair. "It needs a new cushion," she said. "That thing is battered beyond belief. Dad wouldn't let me buy him a new one because it might not have the same padding that Mom sewed into it! Which his bum had worn exactly right."

She chuckled. "Of course he didn't say bum."

"Dad said he wanted me to have it," Harold told his sister.

"He said it was mine," Leonard countered. "He said he'd just use it till he died."

"Who's going to take it then?" she asked.

Leonard grimaced. "That's the point!"

Norma sighed. "Not even cold in his grave and you're fighting over his chair."

"Keep out of it then," Leonard said.

As far as he was concerned, Harold told Norma, they could pack up everything else and give it away.

Leonard stated that he wasn't interested in going through towels and ties either.

"At least you agree on that," she said.

Harold had folded his arms across his chest. "I'm taking the chair," he insisted.

Norma scowled. "Harold. *Really.*" It was meant to remind him that he was the oldest. A minister to boot. Wasn't yielding part of his job?

She sighed again, as if she'd finally comprehended that the spell of their father's passing was over.

Leonard eased himself into the rocker. He began to rock and his face was flushed. He muttered in Harold's direction, "You'll have to take me too."

Norma wanted to laugh but then she noticed Harold moving toward Leonard. She saw that his hands had fisted. They seemed massive in the small, old-fashioned room. The memory of Harold's glorious triumphs in high school track and field events, his muscular stride, his head pitched back and ridged with intensity, shot into her mind as a warning. She was unable to laugh, but she did what she could: she twisted and flung herself into the space between her brothers.

Harold crashed into her. He knocked her against Leonard and she tumbled to the floor.

Norma gasped, but otherwise there was silence. She clambered to her feet, rubbing her elbow. "Good grief," she said.

Harold backed away and Leonard got up. He stood in front of the rocking chair, stiffly, as if at attention.

"A lot of help you two are," Norma said. She pushed her dark, shoulder-length hair behind her ears. "Just get out. I'll sort the stuff already."

The brothers remained.

"Get out," she said. "I don't want the ugly thing but I'll take it myself."

"It's not ugly," Leonard said.

"I take it," she said, "or we turn it into firewood."

Leonard released a low despairing groan, strode to the door, and disappeared.

Norma yanked the green and yellow knitted afghan off the chair and folded it with large, violent motions. She flung the seat cover onto the floor.

"Beat it, Harold," she said. "I'll take care of it."

Harold seemed unsure of himself.

"Well, I mean it," Norma said, "so stand there as long as you want."

Harold finally turned and disappeared after his brother.

Over the next months, Harold and Leonard saw the rocking chair occasionally when they gathered at Norma's house. Friendliness had returned to their interactions and, as always, the families spent time together at Thanksgiving, Christmas, and Easter, and for their combined birthdays in June.

Whenever Harold came into his sister's house he tested himself by looking hard at the chair. He regretted the incident in his late father's apartment. He was glad the chair was still in the family; he was sure he didn't mind that it stood in Norma's family room instead of his own. He felt it giving him another gift. A story was forming around it. The story wasn't ready but it was simmering like a pot of tasty stew.

It was the story of his sister and her brisk, brusque, peacemaking ways. He would mask her identity, of course, and he wouldn't describe the tumble in detail, but the sight of her sprawled there beneath him, blouse askew, breasts slung and vulnerable, had coalesced into a symbol of something both beautiful and profound. A sign of suffering the anger of others. Not passively, but taking a risk. A sign with the power to inspire those who witnessed or heard of it. Someday, perhaps, it would stir his people to acts of reconciliation of their own.

Leonard stole only glances at the chair. In this way, he became aware of its flaws—its scratches, and how years of human skin upon its arms had browned and altered the finish. He'd seen, for the first time, the crack in one of the spindles. He felt that these faults were a help to him, as if the chair itself had come to his aid, had revealed that it was lost and unimportant, and that one should let what was lost diminish and die.

Sometimes, like a recurring painful twitch at the site of an old injury, the summer of making the chair returned to him. The smell of wood at the lathe and the sawdust and oil, the hot buzz and chatter of insect and bird, the shady contrast of the neat garage in which they'd worked, his father's exuberant praise—"The way your hands and head can work together!" As a teen, Leonard thought his father a bit of a fool. But Leonard was newly married when they worked on the chair, ready at last for the older man's zeal, for the approval a father can give.

Leonard told himself that his father had been old and forgetful when he offered Harold the chair. He told himself that a son in the church was something to boast about for his parents' generation. They never lost their awe that his brother had studied at the seminary and taken a pastorate. As far as they were concerned, their prayers had been heard. Leonard told himself the facts.

Each of George Martens's three children spent their small inheritance on travel. Harold and Jean drove through Shield country and into Quebec for two weeks in fall without their children, enjoying the colours and stopping at whim to eat or browse for crafts or secondhand books. Harold said they'd been refreshed; they'd been renewed.

Leonard and Linda took the family to Disneyland. "Blew it all and then some!" Linda glowed. She'd snapped more than two hundred photos, one or another of the children in front of every amusement. She insisted on showing them all.

Norma and Kevin with their Tiffany and Luke camped at Waterton Lakes. "And," Norma said, as if required to account for it all, "we spent the rest on stuff for the house."

She looked at her brothers, kitty-corner at her dining-room table, where they'd just finished their Christmas dessert. She said, "I bought a new cushion for the rocking chair."

Neither brother reacted and Norma decided that neither of them was quite over it yet.

Fire-red cushion notwithstanding, Norma never sat in the chair. It unsettled her with its reminder of her fall. Leonard's bony knees. And Harold's feet. He'd been wearing sandals that day and his toenails were long and rough.

The chair crowded the family room. It didn't fit with the rest of the furniture. She hated it. But she kept it there, as if it was a kind of memorial.

More than a year had passed since George Martens's death, and time had worked no healing magic for Norma and her rocking chair. Every morning, rounding the stairs, it was the first thing she saw. All legs, it seemed, like some gigantic and hideous spider.

She imagined conversations with her father in which she informed him that she despised his chair. In which she blamed him for not being clearer about who was supposed to have it. Bad enough that he'd given away their inheritance, but diluting his legacy because of a chair?

He wore a meek and puzzled expression as she accosted him with her words. He didn't speak. Sometimes his eyes seemed to widen and his lips popped open as if she'd been strangling him. Then she felt sorry. She'd always been kind to him, hadn't she, and efficient? Honouring the domestic concerns of his lonely widower's life? What had he done to warrant her irritation now?

It occurred to Norma one day that he was trying to tell her the chair was none of her business.

That same day, Norma persuaded Kevin to take the kids to the Half Moon for burgers. She wasn't hungry, she said, and it was time for him to bond with his teens.

They left and she phoned to summon her brothers. She untied the red cushion and pulled the chair into the middle of the room. When Harold and Leonard arrived, she made a speech. It was short and crisp.

"I have no idea who should have this chair," she said, "but I'm sure it's not me. It belongs to one of you, so figure it out."

She strode from the room but at the stairs felt overwhelmed by exhaustion. She felt her progress upwards as a crawl. She crept into her bedroom. She closed and locked the door and tottered onto the bed. Any moment now, she would hear the proof of her fears: a lengthy argument, or blows. She remembered her brothers tearing into each other because of a baseball glove, Leonard screaming "I hate you," and Harold taunting, "You stupid little fart." Remembered how conflict galvanized, then drained her; how hard she'd always worked to distract, deflect, cajole, and force them together—or apart. Whatever the circumstances required.

Hadn't their adult friendship been her success as well? Hadn't her knowledge of their history been vital to what they'd all managed to become?

But who—and what—did any of them know? Each knew secrets of their own; that's what they knew. Even good childhoods, she thought, were painful in one way or another. Her brothers' battles had made her stomach ache. Her mother's worries, her nagging over money, had given her stomachaches too.

The bed was relief. Norma's mind began to tumble and fall as if there was nothing to stop it. She tumbled into a strange, bold sleep and when she woke, she realized the house was quiet.

She went downstairs. The rocking chair was gone.

The room where she'd parked it for more than a year seemed to be breathing again. She liked the look of it now, the slightly off-kilter sense of the understated, the under-furnished, the sense of openness a design magazine might consider a muse. She stood at the railing between the family room and the kitchen, taking it in.

The room faced south. Although it got a great deal of sunshine, it seemed even brighter than before.

Not just brighter. Not just spare. Norma could not articulate what else she felt, except that the room seemed—paradoxically —fuller too. More detailed somehow. As if the chair had left behind shadow or some lovely complexity.

My Name Is Magdalena

1.

Mr. Macdonald said, The first sentence is the hardest. He said, Write your name if it helps. You can take it out later. Let's try it aloud, he said. Say your name, say why you're here. Talk about yourselves. We want to get to know each other well this winter, don't we? I was in the front, so I had to start. The room was cold. Everyone else had coffee to hold as a warm bouquet, to lean into and smell. I held an empty notebook. The winter in my fingers was climbing up my arms, aiming for my throat. I spoke quickly, before it got there. I said, My name is Magdalena Wiens. I'm a widow, I think, and I used to clean houses. So much has happened to me.—I wasn't sure, should I go on, should I list what I meant? Mr. Macdonald said, That's wonderful, excellent, a good place to start. I thought he smiled and nodded too much, the way people smile when they don't comprehend what you're saying. Perhaps he noticed my accent. Perhaps he pitied me.

Then the boy behind me said, I'll level with you all. I'm in it for the bucks. I've got talent and I plan to cash it in. Mr. Macdonald said, Excellent, no problem, no problem at all. He said, It's important to be honest.—A girl with long yellow hair opened a folder. These are my poems, she said. She moved her arm and they accidentally slid to the floor. All of us leaned over to pick up her poems. She giggled while we handed them back. She said she was nervous. But the poem that had fluttered under my chair looked as pretty as wash on a washline against a white sky.—I couldn't concentrate. I was the oldest. The only head that was grey. After the class was over, Mr. Macdonald and the others left in a clump. They all seemed to know what writers do. I stayed behind and gathered the paper coffee cups and scraps they'd torn off and played with. I put them in the waste can. I was thinking, I won't be back. But I remembered the advice to begin with my name.

2.

My name is Magdalena Wiens. Voices fill my mind, like a pail at the well. Once they've been heard they refuse to leave. Abram whispers *Magda*. We sat side by side in the garden, on the bench near the summerhouse, which we had wounded by neglect. My father said we shouldn't use the summerhouse because of the troubles in Russia. He broke some windows and splattered the walls with mud. He put on poverty as an overcoat and stored his rubles under bricks and worn boards. He would have lifted his skin for them if possible.—Abram and I were sitting on the bench near the summerhouse, by the cherry bushes. They were thick that year, rosy with harvest. They had no idea of my father's schemes. I felt the layers of leaves beneath my feet and the daylight fading to grey and brown. Darkness wrapped the summerhouse with its merciful shawl and Abram's lips were brushing my ear. His breath was warm. He whispered *Magda*. He always shortened my name and it floated from his mouth like duck's down, over the changes around us. Over the old fallen leaves.

3.

My name is Magdalena Wiens. I've had joys; I've had sorrows. You'll recognize them in everything I say. I was born in 1900, on the 6th of July. Mutti came from a good Molotschna family and a jewel of a village, to hear her speak of it. Her proud heart was a grinding stone when she had to move east of the Urals with Papa. What could she do but complain, recalling what she'd left behind? My father's brothers were going, so he insisted on going too. So they missed the worst of the Revolution. The terrors that befell Ukraine, I mean. Then finally she saw God's hand in the fact of their leaving, of their coming here. But the new Russia eventually reached us too.—I remember Before. I had twenty-five sets of underwear ready for marriage. I sewed them by hand and crocheted lace for their hems. I had a tower of pillows and quilts in my room. My father didn't mind that Abram turned his eye on me, but Mutti was dissatisfied. You're beguiled, she said, because Abram is handsome. He comes from that shiftless clan, those Wienses. They're musical, yes, but every one of them is lazy. He's a lazy sheepskin, you'll see. What did it help? He brought his mandolin. He swept up Mutti's arguments. He shook them into love songs. His music was stronger than her sermons.

45

4.

I remember the moonlight crawling toward me over the floor. The fire had expired, but the moon was bright, the baby asleep in my arms. It had taken me hours to settle him. A child becomes you, my husband said. He bent his head to the boy but one hand plucked at my breast and the other was like a scythe at my thighs. I jerked and hissed at him, I'm pitifully weary, can't you see? I just want to cry. So cry, he said. Now you know what your life will be like. Put him down and cry. The words were hard but the tone not as hard as I'd expected. I began to whimper as if he were an old woman with whom I could share my secrets. I wish I was small again, I said, being rocked to sleep the way I rock our baby boy. Then he laughed.—I remember how easily Abram laughed, how he picked me up, me still cradling the baby. He lifted us easily and carried us both to our beds.

5.

The mandolin soon stood in the corner. A spider anchored a web on its neck. I let it be. I let the dust settle over it too. We were poor and moved back to Ukraine, to a village *kolchose* near Mutti's old home. I'm no kulak, Abram said. Like a boast. He sold the mandolin, but first he blew off the dust and played a final song. It was a dance, he said. He asked me what I thought of it. I answered, And what in our situation would put you in mind of a dance? I also asked, And did you tune the mandolin? He had tuned it well but I wanted to puncture his satisfaction. He swore and left the house with it.—I'd prayed to find Ukraine as Mutti had always described it, but I couldn't see it anywhere. Sadness lay over the landscape like a blanket of soot. We had three sons. Three years in a row, and each of them consigned to the graveyard. Then Abram went to Anna. Her lips were a bowl, brimming red. Like wine. Once he'd said I had a beautiful soul. Now my soul was a shadow in the light of her heavy dark hair and her dark round eyes. In the light of her prettiness. He walked back whistling along the village street.—I never thought about it directly. I was numb. Over and over I said, Gracious Jesus, hear me when I call; God in heaven, have mercy on me.

6.

We had more sons by then. Sons who lived. Hans and Bernhard and Heinrich. I carried them off with me because of the war. But I stumbled as I went because of Abram. I was like Hagar, despised and cast away. I was part of that long furrow of women and old men and children before the German army, retreating. Groaning out of one homeland and into another. The army will guard you home, the German lieutenant said; this setback is not permanent.—They pushed us westward with their losses. Over the Dnieper and beyond. We crept across geography you can study on maps, one hour at a time. We kept searching for the border and the end of fear. My little ones gaped at the sky and sometimes they asked, Will Papa come soon? I said to them, He's busy with the fighting. I said to them, He may be killed. It's as God wills. Their questions were too much for me. I shook Bernhard and said, Stop asking, I've told you as much as I know. He clamped his mouth shut and his brothers sat down beside him, all of them looking at the ground. I was telling myself, if he doesn't die, she'll have him as her husband. I never told the boys of his betrayal.

7.

My name is Magdalena Wiens. My body was bitter but Abram had wanted his farewell. The child we conceived was a riddle like Samson's: something sweet in the carcass of defeat. First she brought me consolation; then she brought me grief. She was very sick and I could not wait for morning, for us to plod ahead for help. Should I have stayed, let the feverish child blaze to death on my lap? I told the boys I'd be back the next day or the next. There was nothing else to do. I walked with her through forests of pine as tall as the walls of the Red Sea when Israel fled. I walked through the night, past fires that flickered for reasons I did not know. For reasons I feared. When I reached the nurses they said, You're just in time. Because of this medicine, the child will live. I returned to our caravan and my other children were gone. No one could tell me what had happened. You know the times we're in, they said, it's war, we're refugees.—This sorrow was as big as a book but all its pages are blank. I can't find any good words to begin. If I'd stayed, I'd know the fate of my sons. If I'd stayed, I would have lost my daughter. Justina. I've tried to compare given with taken. To measure them both. To under-stand. I've tried to set myself free from what I did.—When we arrived where they wanted us, the Germans gave me a coat. I wore it for weeks before I found the gold ring sewn in the lin-ing. I thought it was a miracle that would buy what I needed to discover my boys. Surely they too were in a safe and unexpected place.—I never found them.—Later someone told me the cloth-ing they gave us had come from the Jews who were murdered. I've tried to imagine a woman my size bent over my coat, her coat, concealing the ring. I've tried to imagine what both of us could have done differently.

8.

Mr. Macdonald said, Notice the details. I couldn't concentrate in that class, but now it comes back to me. Notice the details. Did he think I'd been on vacation? We fled. I worried what the horses would eat. Their hooves were unshod, they bled on the cobblestones. I always sang to Heinrich when he cried. *Weisst du wieviel Sternlein stehen?* Do you know how many stars there are? The horizon was in flames. If I stopped singing, Bernhard warbled on. Heinrich had the whooping cough. Hans wasn't well either. I've mentioned Justina, born along the way. We shared the cart with my cousin Susanna and she said, We must lighten our load. As if my ailing children were heavy. I removed the wooden box of plates and cups, a few fine things left me from Mutti. Susanna was angry with the animals. At least we have horses, not oxen, I said. She said, You can thank me for that. Her man was a preacher and banished north. Mine had been seized for the Russian army. We were two miserable women, stinging the other like vinegar.—Later I looked for her too, my dear cousin Susanna, who also disappeared. She disappeared with the boys. I kept Justina safe inside my coat and stared at everyone in freight cars and waiting rooms. I stared at every person I passed. They say Poland is lovely but I can't say for certain. The only landscape I cared about was my sons. When I reached Berlin I wrote Abram a letter. I sent it to the last post I had for him. I addressed the same words to Anna, in case he was there. Forgive me, dear husband, I told him, I've lost our boys. All I have left of yours is the daughter you haven't seen. I cover her ears when the sirens scream.

9.

My name is Magdalena Wiens. Then I came very close to a
world in my mind from which I couldn't run away. I wanted to
fall into it, to be warmed. Beyond the past or the future. Then
somebody pushed me up. I think her name was Helena. She was
young. She had younger brothers and a father feeble from the
former war. I forget her face, her last name. I forget everything
except her patient voice telling me what had happened to others.
She too, she said, she too, and that one there. They have suffered
too. I saw visions while she spoke, God dropping like a stone,
onto the cart my boys had vanished in, dropping like a mother
and locking his knees in the agonies of birth. The anthems of the
wounded, a choir and drums and the sound of marching feet.
His womb flaring open for nothing. Only the smallest, the latest,
swaddled in his skirts. I don't mean I think God is a woman. But
I did see him fall and explode and the blood where he broke.
His rags and the baby. Fires combed the city at night but mornings the streets were still littered with splinters. Helena prodded
me, Get up, get up, get up. She said, You're not the only one,
you know. All of us are scarecrows, limbs a-blow without our
previous flesh.

10.

I must have managed. I boarded trains. I stepped onto a ship. I
remember Montreal, the gleaming windows and the lakes with
shores where no one lived. Trees as cathedrals. I removed myself
somehow from one train after the other, or maybe it was simply
a dream, swaying down the jolting passages of wind, clutching
my daughter's hand. Not so hard, she wailed, you're hurting me.
I cried down to her, I'm sorry, I didn't know I was squeezing,
forgive me darling, does it hurt you very much? I walked and
walked until I found a coach with clean blue seats. I found two

seats banded together by sunshine and then I kissed her and settled her on the cushion beside me, stroking the small hand I had hurt in my desperate, bony grip.

11.

My name is Magdalena Wiens. I've put down the facts as they happened. In Winnipeg, I cleaned for a living. It wasn't as difficult as people imagined. I liked to wash linoleum on my knees. To practise English words as I worked. Teak. Daffodils. Canadian constitution. I liked to be alone in the houses I cleaned, with their layers of drapes and the quiet light. Justina was angry with me once and said, Just because they're rich, just because you're cleaning their houses, doesn't make you as special as they are. She had her times, and I think it was, she had no father, no brothers or sisters, nobody but a mother who worked. It wasn't easy for her, the other girls set in families. I had the trees or the river near. I had the lit kitchen window guiding me home when I stepped off the bus winter evenings. I took in laundry too. I composed lives for my missing sons while I ironed. This shirt belongs to Hans; he's a doctor. A kind German couple raised the boys as their own. I hear Bernhard sing. And his children are blond. I have heirs and some of them resemble me. Only Heinrich stayed small. He shuddered when he coughed. I couldn't visualize anything else for Heinrich, except that his brothers had not abandoned him.—We managed, Justina and I. We filled our little home with the good smell of soap and my baking, and the sounds of her music. I saved and saved and bought a second-hand piano. She's as gifted as her father was. If she has a melody she does what she wants with it.

12.

Every year I made a quilt or two. I collected scraps and stored
them in piles by colour. The piles got as round as vegetables or
fruits and then I preserved them in patterns or puzzles or even
just memories of what we had worn. My stitches were even and
neat. Some quilts I sold and some I gave away. For one of the
auctions I made Log Cabin in beiges and browns. The pieces
were so small it took me all winter. I got tired of it but it fetched
the highest price that year for Mennonite relief. Then I was glad
about the hours that sent grain to the desert. I made a quilt for
Justina with fabric I bought. She thought patchwork was funny:
cutting up cloth to sew it together again. She chose Crossed
Wedding Rings, even though she hadn't married. For myself, I
worked on Trip Around the World with variations. There were
surprises in the rows. Once the lines were set, I didn't rearrange
them. Tiny geese swam between poppies. They lifted their heads
primly, to a red and navy sky.

13.

My name is Magdalena Wiens. There's no end to voices and the
things that people say. To memories. As if distance means nothing. As if thirty good years won't swallow the lean. I'm braid-
ing my hair and I hear him. I'm watering the violets, I think he
has come. He's whispering *Magda*. He's here with the boys. Oh!
They're taller than he is and looking so nice and friendly. But I'm
an old woman and what will they think of me now? No, no. I say
No again. It's only a wish that plays its tricks. So I listen. It's the
mailman on the walk. A sparrow perhaps. Some bird has flown
against the window, believing the reflection of clouds and blue.
There's a fragment of feather on the glass. I search the grass but
the bird isn't there. It might be hurt, if only I could find it, let it

rest in my hands. In the nest of my words. I'd say, I know, I know. Yes, I know. Somebody knows what has happened to you.

Notes for obituary (added by J.)

Magdalena Wiens, born July 6, 1900, to Peter and Katherine (Petkau) Rempel, first of Fischau in the Molotschna of southern Russia and then of Omsk; a happy childhood and youth in spite of the upheavals of the Russian Revolution and World War I; married Abram Wiens in 1924, returned with him to Ukraine; their union blessed with seven children, three of whom died in infancy, three of whom disappeared, one of whom survives her; in World War II, her husband conscripted by the Russians, she sent westward with the Germans; emigrated to Canada in 1948, settling in Winnipeg and working as a housekeeper in several homes until 1971; died suddenly, of heart failure, January 2, 1981; wanted to write her story, so made these notes; feared it might not be believed, though every word, she insisted, was true.

Crucifix on the Road to Gnadenheim

Elinor discovers the crucifx in the *supermercado* while she is looking for soap powder. It stands on the shelf of souvenirs for tourists, towering—perhaps a foot tall—over a dusty assortment of decorative wooden bowls and coasters, tooled leather bookmarks and wallets, key chains, and plaques with bottle trees or oxen painted onto them. These objects, piled haphazardly, look shabby and abandoned, like secondhand merchandise. The *palosanto* crucifix, however, gleams. Its dark green and bronze lines shimmer, as if freshly carved, freshly polished.

So powerful is the impression of its newness, in fact, that Elinor jerks her head toward the aisle, half-expecting to catch a glimpse of someone with a whittling tool darting away. She sees no one, and shakes her head, confused. She turns her attention back to the crucifx.

The hung Christ shudders, curves into the wood. He is dying in front of her. He slumps as gravity demands: his arms distend, his head and legs cave downward, sideways. Then he hangs still, weighted with blood and flesh that has given up.

The paler lines of the wood's grain, sand-coloured, flow along the folds of the cloth over his loins. It makes them ripple a little, as if a chilly wind has begun to blow. The plait of thorns on his head, cut of some contrasting wood, appears to have lifted slightly and seems as light and painless as straw.

But the body may still be warm.

Elinor looks around her. The girls at the checkout tills are busy with customers. Her mother-in-law is at the butcher shop. "I'll meet you at the truck," she had said. Elinor hears the distant whine of a motorcycle and the faint, steady hum of the building's air conditioner. She is alone and unobserved.

She wraps her left hand around the dead man's chest and lifts him down. With her right hand, she cradles the cross. She brings the prone body carefully to her nose. She inhales.

The strong fragrance of *palosanto* rushes into her nostrils.

It rushes in, that sweet brown smell, to comfort her. It makes her think of a mound of ashes bubbling with heat, branches bending low enough to sweep the ground, the shadows of the washhouse at dusk. Elinor closes her eyes. She was dreaming a lovely dream once, wasn't she? Fragments she'd glimpsed as a child and expanded into a story: a home of her own. If only she could remember the dream, remember why it had made her content.

Her hands begin to tremble. Her eyes fly open and she thrusts the crucifix back to its place. She rushes away from it down the aisle to find the soap. She glares at the soap boxes and bottles in front of her until she finally recollects which brand she uses. Oh, she groans, why did I notice, why did I stop, why did I touch it? Is this the way of divine assistance? Or is it the fine art of the devil?

But after she pays for her jar of yogurt, her cheese, sugar, and laundry powder, she is unable to stop herself from circling around to the crucifix again. This time she picks it up with a nonchalant manner, as if merely curious about the price.

The crucifix is expensive. It would cost her far too much. Elinor hurries away a second time, ashamed.

She stops the truck in front of her mother-in-law's house. She carries in the other woman's groceries. When she steps into the kitchen, she feels its wonderful coolness. The room seems completely detached from the midday heat.

Elinor's mother-in-law is stout but very energetic. She hurries into her bedroom to change her clothes. "Have you seen how full the lemon tree is?" she calls from around the corner. "Ronald loves lemon juice. Especially when it's fresh."

The older woman emerges in a clean, faded home dress of light brown cotton. "We should work in the garden this afternoon," she says, tying an apron around her waist.

Elinor smiles her acquiescence, because that's what she did at the beginning, when she wanted so badly to learn. She has been unable to stop answering this way, even though each smile uses up her life as breathing uses air. She wishes she could lie down on the table in her mother-in-law's kitchen, on the calm blue oilcloth with the white sailboats floating across it. But she smiles and nods, and Ronald's mother says, "We'll see you later then."

Elinor drives the truck several hundred feet further, parks beside the old house where she and Ronald live. When they married, they built a house for his mother in a corner of the *Hof*, close to the street. The mother's house is small but, in the manner of the newer homes, has a wide verandah and modern conveniences—an indoor toilet, a gas stove, glass windows, kitchen cupboards. Elinor's house strives to keep up-to-date through her constant scrubbing, but this is a battle that cannot be won; hers is a house mutinous with ancient construction and creaking inefficiencies.

Elinor puts the provisions away. She writes down, in Ronald's accounting book, the sum that she spent. Ronald is at their ranch land and will not be home for dinner, so she undresses without eating and lies down on their bed for siesta. The shutters are closed; the room is dark and hot and airless. She doesn't have the strength to get up and turn on the oscillating fan.

The desperation is with her again: the familiar and painful desperation. How to describe it, even to herself, this sense that she is disappearing, that she is drying and cracking? It isn't the weather, or a lack of physical health, but some other seepage she cannot plug.

She came from the other side of Paraguay to marry him, to live with him here on the farm, in the farming village of Gnadenheim. His village name meant "home of grace" in German, Ronald told her after they met in the capital, after they had fallen in love. With words like these, he persuaded her and she came, leaving father and mother, brothers and sisters and friends. She became Mennonite for him, instead of Catholic. She unpacked herself as a box. She yielded herself as a garden does to the plow, to seed and sun and rain.

She had not known what it would cost to be a stranger. She had not known how difficult and dangerous it would be. Boldly she had seized the words of Ruth as her own—*Where you go, I will go. Where you lodge, I will lodge. Your people, my people. Your God...*

But these words no longer travel through her mind in sentences. They are hard, separate entities now—*where*, and *you*, and *I*, and *go*, and *lodge*. They are not fluid as before, not linked to pull her from peril.

Nor can she make her husband comprehend her despair. People are amazed how well you fit in, he replies affably, how hard you work; and isn't everyone very nice, trying their best? One should not mind what people think, he says, and when Elinor assures him this isn't the problem, he looks victorious, as if that's exactly what he wanted her to get the knack of. One day he reveals he's been grateful she's quiet: two talkative women on one *Hof* would be too much for any man, he says, but he offers this sheepishly, like a basket of grapefruit stolen from a neighbour's tree.

All Elinor has to offer is herself, whenever he wants her. She thinks that if they had a child she would feel better, but this has not happened. She clings to Ronald long after he falls asleep, tearfully stroking his rough, sun-reddened face.

In spite of everything, she is alert to omens of help. The crucifix must be a sign. It will not let her rest. She calculates how many eggs she will have to sell, how many weeks it will take in order to buy it. She investigates the house and the barn for a hiding place.

On the next week's trip into town, Elinor wanders to the tourist shelf to reinforce the hopes she is weaving together. The souvenirs are as dishevelled and untended as before, all of them bleating *Recuerdo del Paraguay* in gold-ink lettering under a fine layer of dust. Souvenirs of Paraguay, indeed. But the crucifix is gone.

Had she dared to think it would wait for her? That it would repeat INRI—Jesus of Nazareth, King of the Jews—with its quiet assurance and power to other customers until she was ready to take it home? Just because there weren't many tourists visiting the Chaco, just because Mennonites didn't use crucifixes, just because the Catholic Indians were very poor?

How foolish she was, how naïve, to suppose it would not be snatched away. To suppose it was safe. Intended for her!

She slouches away from the gaping shelf, disappointment dropping into her stomach like a stone.

The following week, Elinor notices that, from a distance, one of the electrical posts along the road to Gnadenheim resembles a crucifix.

Ronald is driving—he needed to pick up some parts for the tractor—and he and his mother are discussing the crops. The peanuts are doing better than the castor-oil plants, he says; he might have proportioned the land a little differently, instead of half and half, but still, they're all looking good enough so far and he's satisfied. He's certainly not sorry he dropped cotton. The crucial factor, of course, is rain. If the fields don't get rain, within a week for sure, the damage will be severe.

Elinor spots it just past the bend in the road, the bend a mile or so from the village, where Ronald says the horses pick up speed and run home in earnest. The expression comes from his late father, from the days of wagons and buggies. This crucifix is large, and it's approximate, but once she sees it, it cannot be denied. Trees in the Chaco side of Paraguay are neither tall nor straight enough to serve as posts for the electrical lines, so the best of the yellow *quebracho* trunks, crooked as they are, are used in twos. They're fastened together with a metal belt to form a single post. In the bottom trunk of the post, Elinor sees the heavy, downwardly-curved shape of the crucified legs; in the upper, the torso. The cross beam with its bracing suggests the saviour's stretched-out arms. A huge parrots' nest woven over the top forms the head, and its crown of thorns.

For the first time in many months Elinor comes close to laughing. For a moment, she catches the irony, that she has been reduced to sustenance from such a crude and patched-together gesture, that in this community with its stark religiosity, she is allowed only icons of nature, those formed of coincidence, of survival in a desolate place and the whims of a colony of birds.

By the time the truck stops at their house, her amusement has vanished; the crucifix she was given on the road has solidified, is sufficient. When she steps into the kitchen, she is startled by a voice. A preacher is calling. "Bring all of your sins and your burdens! Bring them all to the foot of the cross!"

Ronald has left the radio on again.

Everyone is waiting for rain. Everyone watches the sky, and the life is disappearing from Elinor's body. She is unable to convince her husband that she is afraid. She is sure she has spoken plainly more than once, but her statements, it seems, are plain to her alone; why else do they cause him no alarm?

She has wrestled with her new situation a long time, but now she is mortally weary; she wishes to surrender. She feels her efforts slacken, preparing to succumb.

No rain has fallen, the crops suffer on. Ronald is angry. Elinor's mother-in-law is ill with a flu. She hands Elinor her grocery list and says, "I know I'd recover if the weather would turn."

Elinor sets out for town, alone in the old red truck. It's a bright, nearly white day, and very hot. A car passes her, churning up dust, but Elinor drives into the billows of fine grey sand without slowing. She anticipates the crucifix waiting for her beyond the bend, sagging with sorrow: her image of consolation. She imagines herself aiming for the place where the Christ-legs cross. She imagines *quebracho*—nearly indestructible—and metal meeting with a crack, an anguished cry, and blood. She imagines being finished.

Around the curve of the road, she sees two men from the municipality doing maintenance work on the lines. They've knocked the nest off her post, and she gasps; the crucifix has been undone. Then she thinks of the parrots, turned out of their home. Parrots are pests. They'll be gathered in a tree somewhere, squawking and screaming their displeasure, planning to rebuild.

Elinor wants to laugh, and this time, she lets herself. It feels sweet in her throat. It feels like air.

Postponement

Shelley Henderson leans against the wall in the shade of the Medical Arts Building for a good half hour after her appointment is over, considering what to do next.

She decides she won't say the words *my cancer* aloud to anyone yet. Not even David. He doesn't know she's been seeing the doctor or having tests, so there are no questions to answer. Surely she can wait a few hours before rushing home to tell him. Surely she can gather her breath.

She begins to walk then, up Kennedy Street, west on Graham, suddenly buoyed by her resistance to what she'd assumed the moment Dr. Joss gave her the diagnosis, that she had to get out of the office immediately and speak to her husband. It seems a victory now, this postponement, these snatched hours to think. To ponder what lies before her, what lies behind.

Shelley enters the Bay, takes the escalator to Stationery. She buys a journal book with a linen wine-coloured cover and heavy unlined paper, and a package of blue ink-jet pens: medium-tipped, not micro. David uses micro and his writing, she thinks, looks spidery.

Next, she goes to Lingerie. She wants a new nightgown, something cozy and warm—because the air conditioner runs nearly all summer—but good-looking too. And she finds it: a long gown in antique white, soft to the wrists, soft to the neck, stretchy but flowing, the bodice embroidered in tiny white flowers. The gown is expensive but this doesn't stop her today.

She takes her purchases to the store cafeteria where she orders a cheeseburger with everything but onions. While eating, she anticipates beginning her journal. It gives her pleasure to think of it. Soon her emotions, opinions, strategies, and lists will be set down in one place. Saved. They won't be eloquent; she's no writer of stories and poems. But she'll have something. A small archive of words.

After her lunch, Shelley removes her tray to an empty table and opens her book to the first page. On the top line she writes the date, on the next:

Today I found out I have cancer.

She leaves a line and writes:

Decisions I have to make:

1. Which of the treatment options I want.

2. How to organize my time around it.

Shelley sucks on the end of her pen. She has run out of critical issues already. She is startled at how few they are. It had seemed that her mind was reeling with them.

Then she remembers.

Decision already made: don't tell anyone, not even David, until I've had some time to brood on it.

The page is not even half full. The rest of it tantalizes her with its lovely emptiness, invites her to blue it. She continues.

After Alegra disappeared I plunged in. Immediately, and with everything I had. Talking, talking, talking. Then I was stuck in the middle of all that sound. My voice, and their voices. I felt stabbed by their support instead of cushioned. Deflated. Every sentence another nail. If I was worried or overwhelmed, they said look on the bright side. If hopeful or cheerful, even forgetting for a while, they said it was strange to be happy, wasn't I just terribly sad and unsettled? I lost myself and not just my daughter in that maze of commiserations, advice, invitations to spill my soul. The grief I'd already been carrying around about me and David just got worse and I never heard his voice at all. This time, I want to start another way.

David sees Shelley in the new nightgown and before he can stop himself he's blurted, "Wow, you're beautiful!" He intended to think before he spoke, to search his mind whether he had seen the gown already, or consider at least what she wanted to hear, what might be construed by his words. He's spent a lifetime of marriage, it seems to him, getting the compliments wrong. Not enough of them, for one thing, or too many remarks implying he'd never noticed a piece she'd owned for months. Or getting the slant of it wrong, too much emphasis on the garment itself, not enough on the woman inside it. Or vice versa. He does his best, he always insists, though he knows he lapses into self-pity when he is misunderstood.

Its whiteness has shocked him, that's all, and the breadth of its whiteness. It covers her completely, nothing showing but her bare feet at one end and her head at the other. Even her hands have vanished in the long creamy sleeves, though now she's folding up the cuffs, her long fingers emerging. The fabric doesn't cling as much as wrap her, like a shroud, but it shows her figure well enough. She's been trying to lose weight and he thinks she may have dropped a few pounds. He's attempted to convince her that she suits him just the way she is, but she doesn't believe him. She's larger, yes, than when they met, but she's grown on him and he wants to say he likes it. But that will surely come across as careless and worn as their relationship has become over the years. Except that she keeps surprising him by how quickly hurt she is, by her sensitivity. There are days he feels he should tiptoe around her, or disappear altogether.

"Thanks." She lifts her head. She's smiling slightly, seems amused. Tolerant.

"You've been cold, I guess," he says, meaning it as an apology for his fussiness over how the air conditioner is set. "It looks like you're geared up for winter."

"I needed something new."

"It's different than your pajamas. What you usually wear, I mean. That's why I said that."

"Said what?"

"That you're beautiful."

"Didn't you mean it?"

"I did. But it just came out. I meant the gown is very beautiful. You're beautiful inside it. Without it too."

It makes her giggle.

When she steps toward him, he puts his arms around her and feels her laughter, the fabric, her body against him. He's glad that his comment succeeded. But he doesn't know why he succeeded this time when he fails so often.

Love is entanglement. Last night, of the body. He said, afterwards, in his blunt way, "I could go to heaven on that." I woke up later; it was something like 2 a.m. The back yard was lit by a moon that was nearly full. The world seemed dark and at the same time shining and I felt we should be out there having a conversation, about our bodies or souls or something. But I had left him sleeping and since I haven't told him yet, it would have been silly to wake him. I won't tell him while he's tired or half asleep. I pinched off the dead petunias in the boxes he's built around the deck. They curve as

*they die, become narrow and papery. Is the difference between life
and death just moisture then?*

*I haven't cried yet. I suppose I'm in denial, in shock, not com-
prehending, not getting it. But I said "Me too" after his comment,
and usually I just can't speak after sex. I don't think I'm in denial.*

Since she's postponed it for one day, it's easy to postpone telling
David for two. Why spoil the barbecue they planned weeks ago,
with Lorraine and Ralph, Tom and Holly?

In the morning he urges her not to fuss, their friends will
be fine with chips and bread. He'll buy and flavour and sear the
meat, to everyone's specifications. As he always does.

"Chips with steak? David, we've discussed this before."

"It's the summer holidays."

"Those massive slabs of beef are a waste of money and not
terribly satisfying food-wise either. Please allow me my salads."

"Didn't you say the war on red meat was a feminist plot to
render men completely docile? Didn't you use the words, the
sabotage of salads?" He's grinning.

"I'll have steak, David. A small one to be sociable. But really,
it's no big deal to make a potato salad. To cut veggies and fruit."

"We should explore the gender connotations of food."

Shelley doesn't respond. Suddenly the exchange seems nonsensical, as if preserved in cartoon bubbles over their heads. One
of a long row of nonsensical conversations. Dabs of superficial
words, used as a salve for the pain between them. She's low on
energy for banter today, annoyed with him. Who cares whether
food has sexist connotations, how it fits into the gender wars?
There are probably dissertations on these topics somewhere; let
the academics stew over them.

In the evening, she greets Lorraine and Ralph with a warmth
that seems relief, as if she'd been anxious over them, although, in

fact, she wasn't thinking of them at all. Lorraine has a new dress, in cranberry tones. She looks lovely, as usual.

Tom and Holly arrive minutes later and Shelley relaxes completely. Holly is vivacious. She'll carry the conversation if required. Everyone likes Holly.

These couples stuck closest to them through their daughter's escapades and her death. Even Tom, the quiet one, whom Shelley had actually once been afraid of, thinking he didn't like her. And then he showed up every day while they looked for Alegra. He did the dishes and vacuumed, which confused Shelley, and embarrassed her, until she asked him, please would he stop, and he said, okay, he would. He said he hated housework but he was a practical man and didn't know what else to do to let her know that he cared, since there was nothing to fix around their place. And Shelley had sighed, "I know," as if it was a burden for both of them, and she said, "But now I got the message you care, so you can quit," and in the look that flashed between them there was real affection, and the hint of desire.

They had not looked away, but let it heat to hunger, and then they had fallen upon each other with a fervour Shelley was unable later to trace, in spite of how distinct it had been, and nearly unstoppable. She'd been certain by then that Alegra had overdosed but she didn't think about Alegra while they embraced, kissed, and groped toward coupling, ready to bolt to the bedroom in a rush of need and release. Until some horror at what they were doing sparked them apart, muttering apologies. They could hardly grasp their betrayal, to Holly and to David. They vowed their silence, their formal distance. The same distance as earlier.

The friends discuss their children again. David made the speech at last summer's barbecue: the rest of them should not consider their children off limits out of respect for their loss. They would not be hurt, he said, and Shelley concurred, though she found herself less able than she'd expected to endure the resumption of parental news, the banalities, the boasts and complaints.

This evening, a great deal of time is taken up with Tom and Holly's Darrin, and his crazy experiences with vehicles. Fender benders and tickets. "Etc., etc.," they say, before recounting another of his escapades.

Etcetera. Shelley plays with the word in her mind. Other things, unspecified. More of the same. The children of these friends are good kids, decent, ordinarily decent, not distinguishing themselves by first-class achievements, but not by large rebellions either. The extremes have been their domain, hers and David's. Their son Jeff was a star in soccer and volleyball throughout high school and university and his academic achievements were featured in the local paper. Then he'd won a Rhodes Scholarship.

And Alegra? She was always running away.

Holly changes the conversation. "This is the year, guys," she announces. "For the Mexico holiday."

"This is the year," Ralph echoes.

It's a continuing story, this wish of theirs to spend a week in Mexico together once all the children are old enough to be left on their own.

Everyone but Shelley chimes in and soon they're talking as if they will go, this year for sure. She hears David's enthusiasm on behalf of them both, taking her agreement for granted.

"I don't know as I want to be away over Christmas," she finally says.

"Weren't you the one who suggested Christmas?" Holly cries. "Originally?"

"Yeah. But now I can't imagine it," Shelley says. She's imagining herself in a hospital bed, tubes feeding her veins, Christmas carols piped into the room.

But her objection has been too mild. The others ignore it. Shall they go to Acapulco, Puerto Vallarta, Ixtapa? Or one of the newer resorts?

"I'll get some information," Holly volunteers.

"We can't wait too long before booking," says Lorraine. "You know how quickly the best places are taken."

Mutters of assent as a conclusion. The topic shifts again.

Later, when Shelley and David are alone in the gazebo, extending the evening with another glass of wine, Shelley says, "I know I've always wanted to go to Mexico for Christmas, but now I just can't get excited about it."

"Shelley, that's so typical." His voice sounds taut and she wonders if he's bothered by something she did or said during the evening. "You want something until it comes right down to it and then you don't."

He waits a moment and his tone turns pleading. "I'd really like to do it. Make it a Christmas gift for ourselves."

She wants to say, "I may be close to dying then." But she hasn't told him about the cancer yet and the sentence is absurd on its own. Its melodrama offends her. She might not be anywhere close to dying. It shouldn't be assumed, Dr. Joss told her, that cancer leads to death. Not nowadays.

So here, Shelley thinks, is my perfect opportunity.

But she says, calmly, as if she's bored with it, "Well, we've got time, don't we? Even if Lorraine doesn't think we do. And you know how Tom and Holly are, they'll go home, remember the cost and change their minds. So I'm not going to get excited."

"But we could go anyway, Shelley. You and me. I want to spend Christmas in Mexico. Just once, a green Christmas. Heat. Ocean and palm trees. Just once, coming back to school with a tan and all the teachers and kids thinking, look at that, he's been away, the principal must make a lot of money!"

It makes him chuckle, and Shelley laughs too.

This moment would be even better for her announcement, but it seems too precious to mar. There's insect-buzz in the warm dark night, and at a distance, the drone of traffic on the ring road. She hears the intermittent call of the mourning dove, the wind rising in the oaks around the gazebo. She listens to the light rhythmic wheeze of her garden rocking chair. Tomorrow, she thinks. Maybe tomorrow.

From my book of names. Shelley means "from the meadow on the ledge." David means "beloved one." His name is old and seems solid and powerful. It never goes out of fashion. Mine comes and goes, it's a movie star name. I never liked it much. I made up Alegra, or perhaps I heard it. It's not in the book and that disappointed her. I told her it was like "allegro," the musical term, brisk and lively, but with the softer feminine "a" at the end and just one "l" for her uniqueness. My explanations never satisfied her. Jeffrey means "divinely peaceful."

"David, David, I've got an idea." David felt Shelley shaking him awake before he heard her words clearly.

"What time is it?" he grumbled.

It wasn't that early, she told him, she'd been up for hours. She'd just had the most exciting idea, she said. What if they packed up and drove out to visit Jeff and Simone? Was there anything on their schedule that couldn't be put off for a couple of days?

"I've booked some golf games," he said.

"You can golf there," she countered. "I just want to lay eyes on them."

There was no good reason not to go, he thought, only the

dread of driving. By the time he was fully awake, he was willing. Even for the driving.

He was more than willing, David thought as he showered. The urgency, the unpredictability. Vintage Shelley, and it pleased him. The qualities that infuriated him when they were younger seemed almost welcome now, given their absence. They aroused his nostalgia. He and Shelley backpacked through Europe like so many of their generation, but nobody's route, he was sure, had been as illogical as theirs. Plotted on the map, it was a series of crazy zigzags. She would wake, early, in the tent or hostel, lie there waiting for him to finish sleeping, and *the most hare-brained idea*—her expression—would come into her head. She received the idea like divine inspiration.

"I just had the most harebrained idea," she would say when he opened his eyes, her long hair in his face.

"We've got to go back to Paris," she'd said in the silliest episode of them all. "I'm not in the mood for Rome. Not yet."

"But we're in Florence. We're practically there. We'd decided to do Italy next."

David could still recall the argument that followed. How she won it. Of course. How they used their rail pass to travel north to Paris and a week later, south again, to Rome.

She'd always laughed over her penchant for changing their plans. She let herself be faulted if the alterations disappointed them, but she never showed remorse. Not when they were young. A shrug, a hint of sheepishness, an outburst of kisses: that was as close as she came to saying sorry.

The golf games, David thought, would be easy enough to cancel. The return of her spontaneity seemed significant.

And so they're driving to Calgary to visit son Jeffrey and his girlfriend Simone. The doctor's receptionist was short with her when Shelley rescheduled her next appointment but Shelley said, "A week's not the end of the world. Take it or leave it." As if she was doing them a favour by coming at all.

How many times have she and David made this trip westward during twenty-nine years together, both their families living in Alberta? That interminable trip, but one she's always loved, though it was hard to keep the children occupied when they were small. Today, the broad flat land as attractive to her as always, particularly green this year, and the sky very blue, loaded with the huge flat-bottomed clouds that appear in postcard images of the prairie, the endless asphalt coiling out ahead of them like a promise.

Sometimes they listen to the radio. Sometimes they use the towns and villages they pass through to pose challenges to themselves. *Grenfell*. Eight words of eight letters beginning with G. *Ernfold*. Seven words of seven letters beginning with E. Sometimes they read aloud, this time *Endurance*, the saga of Ernest Shackleton and his ill-fated sailing ship, which Shelley grabbed in haste from the coffee table stack.

They avoid, as they have for years, the accusations that lead to arguments, and topics that will remind them of the old fights. They no longer speak deeply about themselves. But travelling, shut up close together, lulled by moving, with a common purpose, a common destination, it seems to Shelley that everything deep and unsaid between them is both suggested and resolved. An illusion perhaps, but one she hangs on to, and will not examine or test.

She has decided she'll tell David her news while they travel. She connects her resolve to places, to signs of what's coming: Headingley, Portage la Prairie, Brandon, Alexander, Oak Lake. Once we're *there*, she tells herself, but then they reach that place and she squanders the moment, using any excuse that presents itself, until they reach Regina and she realizes she has no desire to ruin this trip with talk of a disease and its many implications. She wants the sight of Jeff looking well, and hopefully happy, and a look at his new Simone. Just that.

But she doesn't understand her reluctance. Her reasons for not telling David keep shifting in front of her, mutating. Is it revenge for all he's neglected to say? Or has she come to believe in what he practises himself, and calls a virtue: always keeping his own counsel, as he puts it, until he grasps both the problem and solution, giving nothing away until he knows everything he needs to know?

They're just past Medicine Hat, in Alberta, heading home. They agree that they had a wonderful time. Jeff was busy but they managed some meals together, a trip to the zoo, a few hours in Banff. They agree that they like Simone.

Shelley pulls out her journal.

David asks, "Since when are you keeping a diary?"

"It's more like a journal."

"Whatever. You've never done that before, have you?"

"Once. When I was sixteen. Crushes in all their detail. I threw it away when I read it later."

"So what are you writing now?"

"Oh I don't know. Bits and pieces. Reflections, I guess."

"So have you put down how we met? Memories of us?"

"No," she says. "No, I haven't. I'm not writing an autobiography."

She had taken out the journal to describe the brown and goldenrod hues of southern Alberta. But now she thinks about his question. She writes:

In the library, University of Manitoba, all the carrels full, that time in the term when everyone was anxious, and serious. Late evening, fluorescent lights humming over my head, my eyes burning. Two guys in the carrels adjacent discussing calculus, like some foreign language to me. I was trying to write a paper—and I couldn't concentrate because I was tired and they were talking. I couldn't follow their conversation but I couldn't help listening either, enough to know one of them didn't have a clue and the other—David—knew it backward and forward. He explained it. Patiently. I could tell he was going at the same concept from one angle and then another and then another, and scribbling on paper and all of a sudden I heard the other guy saying "Oh, oh, oh!" with that recognition every teacher waits for. I had pushed my chair back and turned my head, curious about his obvious pleasure over catching on, finally, and David looked up at that moment and our eyes met and we grinned our happiness for David's accomplishment, and I saw his perfect teeth. I thought how well they matched his smart and patient voice. Then when we were packing up, because the library was closing, we had to say something on account of that connecting grin. He said, "I hope we weren't bothering you," and I said, "You should be a teacher, you're really good," and he said, "That's what I've been told. I'm resisting it though." He walked with me out of the building. He said, "But since you've suggested it too, maybe I ought to switch to Education." Then he asked, did I want to come for a drink, tell him what I was working on, or trying to at least, while they'd been disturbing me? We talked for hours. I felt us yearning for each other, though we didn't touch. Our words were enough for a good beginning.

—Amazing we're still together. But here we are, post Jeffrey, post Alegra.

She's writing and David says to her, "Don't forget to put down that you're a good mother."

Shelley feels her breath stopped in her body, not moving.

"Present tense, David?" she manages, after a moment. "I'm more or less finished."

"Okay." Affably. "So you were a good mother. You were especially good with Alegra."

"David, don't just say things out of the blue. You've never said that before."

"Sure I have." His voice is sharp with offence. "And I mean it."

"No, you haven't."

"I've always thought it. Especially with Alegra."

The road blurring, heat shimmering in the distance. "Oh David," she bleats at him, "you have no idea how often I could have used that compliment. That one compliment!"

"I'm sure I've said it. I've certainly thought it." Now his tone is casual, confident, covering his indignation.

Back in Winnipeg, back in their own bed, Shelley wakes with the sun, but strangely. She crawls out of a dream as if through a tunnel, struggling to know where she is, what's real, and remembering that she had just achieved something difficult and important. A fragment of it floats toward her. She had said, "Something's wrong, darling," and David had said nothing at all. So typical, she had thought, critiquing him even in a dream, the man who could explain the fine points of mathematics, a philosophy of education, but never say what she needed to hear. But at some point, she remembers, he was holding her and she had perceived what he meant through his hands on her back.

It was a dream but she feels that it happened and all she has to do now is bring it to pass.

The next morning she records it.

His favourite supper, lasagna and caesar salad. Chocolate cake. Wine. The pink tablecloth and matching napkins, candles, the china. Music. As if to be romantic! Though I had no appetite at all. Just before dessert, just after he'd poured the coffee, while he was tipping cream into his cup, I told him. "There's a name for the weariness, you know. For my various symptoms. It's cancer."

I was looking down at the creamer most of the time, ashamed by my news. He stood up and came around to my side of the table and just said "Shelley." Mournfully. I hated to hear it, like a rerun of our earlier griefs. But then it seemed my dream took over and the comfort of his hands closed tightly around me.

In the Village of Women

Down the elevator and out the door she'll be, into the cold and then off to Toronto, maybe for a year and maybe forever, she said. That's what they do nowadays, young people, they move around. She walked away after their tea time, tall and straight as she'd been told, and then at the end of the hallway, she turned and gave a tiny wave, like the wave of a queen, but humorous, it seemed, not fussy.

They'd been oddly shy at first, Ava not saying much besides her news about leaving but smiling that wise steady smile of hers, and the winter sun warm through the windows, the little apartment lapping the light like kittens at milk. Her eyes were summer-blue and clear again, the way they'd been when she was a girl. They were clouded for a while, maybe four or five years, some uncertainty, confusion, the fault of the teens she'd thought it, but freed now and open like a mirror. And tall and straight she'd walked away as she'd been told, like a fine strong stream down the long worn hallway.

It's all she wants Ava to remember, how she herself walked

down a village street, head high, back straight, and how it was the best and hardest thing she'd ever done. Though she'd wondered if it was wrong, her using that word, wondered if straight might be a wound, but then she'd used it again and again because she couldn't think how to say what she needed to say without it or how words sounded when they changed their meanings, English hard enough for her in any case.

Ach Ava, she had said, sighing, *Mein Kind, mein Kind,* my child, yes, but it was her example that mattered, the most difficult walk of her lifetime, no more than ten minutes perhaps, striding down the sandy street, hot and unending under a sun that boiled up mornings to nearly unbearable by noon, and all the other women in their yards by then, watching, she imagined, though she wouldn't look to the left or to the right. Strange how the body could be the sign of everything important. Which didn't mean she wasn't humiliated or hurt.

And Ava had said, Yes, Oma, I know. As if she'd always known that the world was a street, that people lined up on the sides of it. Cheering if you were lucky, and just staring or jeering if you weren't. If they wanted you to be different than you are.

She knows what Ava is. Daughters Esther and Erna sailing in to do a thorough cleaning of her place, and now she knows that Ava is gay. Strange too, such a word, hearing them whisper it while she went down for a nap, Erna tucking her in like an infant, the cool touch of her hand to her cheek, and low voices in the other room, sighs and rustlings like the wind, and she awake too soon, or perhaps not even falling asleep, a-creep out of her bed, listening to her daughters. She listened and the words, though quiet, were crow caws in her ears: *Ava,* and *out,* and *gay,* and *orientation.* And then she remembered the veil of her granddaughter's eyes, knew why it was gone, her gaze so fresh again in its soft calm blue, though there was surely still some tremble there, like a gauzy curtain played by a breeze.

There was tremble in her at least, hearing Esther say there's no use telling Mother, she wouldn't understand, and you know how she is, she's bound to say something inappropriate, some pious pep talk that won't change a thing. Her Esther sounding as bitter as a sink full of dishes. Too religious, they supposed, but she'd never uttered a word on the topic, had she ever? She wanted to spring out and say Boo and wither them with the fact that it was being religious that made her fond of the child in the unrelenting, never-changing way she was fond of her.

So they'd sipped at their tea while she told Ava what ran through her head, walking down the street that day, and it was *yea though I walk through the valley,* she said. The roadway flat as a floor, no valley but for those mountainous eyes looming around her, everyone knowing more than she did perhaps. And less. *Through the valley of the shadow of death...* the shadow... Come to think of it, more shade would have been nice. They weren't joking when they said the Paraguayan Chaco was a hell. A green hell, though, except when it was dust-covered and dry. Wearing her best brown dress that morning, with its pattern of gold circles and squares, which had passed its better days in Germany and came to her secondhand, far too fancy for an over-lit day, for light-coloured soil, for betrayal. She refused a hat in that heat, so young and foolish she was. And proud. The hem of that dress bouncing around her legs like exclamations.

Three years ago now, Ava begging her to write out her life and Erna and Ava's mother Esther there as well, saying, Yes, yes, an excellent idea, Mother, it will give you something to do. She had an Ivan Rebroff record on the player and her daughters were offering her their kind and judging smiles: Mother and her old-fashioned tastes, playing those records. It's how his voice takes her back to her childhood, a happiness too hidden then, slipping out of the fur coats of his songs and the silhouettes of foreign churches. Even in Winnipeg, their onion domes and snow tumbling around them like salt for their beauty, their colours, their melodies, their Ukrainian words.

Please, Oma, she'd said in her pleading voice, such a cozy-in-her-lap until she was twelve or so, and then she was off it, never sitting there again, just part of every sport imaginable which they invited her along to watch sometimes, soccer in the summer and basketball and volleyball the rest of the year, and even in university, she's been on the teams. Only her voice still a curl-up against her shoulder. Write down your life, she'd begged. Everything.

Everything? She was flattered. Even the first engagement, short as it was? Then Esther's look, like a turn, and Erna's jump-in, Don't tell me you're still holding a candle for *him*. And so she'd left all of that out, those six weeks, and the way she'd wound up the flaming yellow ribbon of that disapproving street. Her daughters knew the gist of it already, and they simply couldn't abide her setting it down in black and white, as if it meant she'd loved their father less than she should have. As if perfection is what daughters can demand of their mothers.

You'll have to write about Paraguay, her Esther had said, of course you will, that's where you and Papa met. If it wasn't for Paraguay, we wouldn't exist. Her subsequent laugh a spray of alyssum, so pretty, so unencumbered. She'd rewritten some of the pages a good many times before she was satisfied and Esther made copies for all of them to read. And later Ava said she'd liked it very much and gave her a hug.

Stunned around the corner then, gathering that Esther found it hard and that Erna was a comfort, such good sisters they'd always been for each other, adapting and brave as she'd trusted them to be, in spite of their tiny mockeries, Rebroff and his big head and his beard and his voice of so many octaves between the high and the low, as if he were a clown instead of a mira-cle, and assuming she couldn't handle this, and wouldn't know anything either. She didn't know enough, not the words that cut and the ones that wouldn't, but she watched Oprah, didn't she, and Ellen? She knew a few things about the world. She'd trudged out of Russia beside her mother, lived in the camps, crossed the ocean by ship. Lived in the hell of the Chaco for years she still remembered very well. Moved to Canada.

Of course it was a shock. Every clip of dreams and expectations is a shock and she can't say she wasn't numbed for a while, like Paul on the way to Damascus, first a kind of blindness and then seeing everything new, and not without a certain amount of weeping and praying either, but one got used to it, just as Esther and her good man Alfred had, and Erna and William.

But today, Ava here for a visit and tea, she needed to tell her the piece of her life she'd left out of the twenty-five pages. They'd reached across the table to hold hands for a moment, and then they let go, and she said, Ava, please eat some more, please. The plate with the jam jams and fudge was piled and lonely and she'd hardly touched it. And Ava laughed and said, My brothers will, and my cousins.

The trouble is how much history, how much geography, it takes to make sense of her story. She had to start with Russia and the Revolution, even though she'd written it down, why her grandparents didn't escape when the others escaped, all those misadventures in Moscow, and then her grandfather taken and her father after that, and how she had no memories anywhere left of him, she the second youngest and her brother in the cradle, crying the night they took him away and she as silent as a doll, her mother said. The thirties then, the culls, the persecution, the hunger, and then the Second World War and really, you needed a map to make it plain, how the Germans advanced, and how they retreated.

Then the flight with her mother, her sister pregnant but not with her disappeared husband. Her sister was beautiful, and that's how it was, her beauty had given them seats on a train to be sent into Germany, and then they lost her older brother to the German army, her mother never reconciled to that. Roosevelt, Stalin, and Churchill grinning at one another in Yalta while they divided Europe, but they'd been lucky, they'd found the Mennonite Central Committee or the Mennonite Central Committee found them and then they found themselves free and on their way to South America, though it wasn't so wonderful actually, starting up in Paraguay, the heat and insects as thick as the rubble of Berlin.

The main thing was, they weren't returned to Russia. It was like the man who said he kept a picture of Stalin in his mind, Father Stalin murdering his children by the millions, and then he could swallow his beans and rice, and rice and beans, with gratitude, and didn't mind so much that he was sweating like a horse by nine o'clock in the morning, planting peanuts and cotton instead of wheat. Not to mention digging wells, building houses, you name it.

Her older sister and her mother wanted to be part of the *Frauendorf*, the village of women, and later that Mr. Peter Dyck and his Elfrieda who helped with the transport, said it probably had no precedent, a Mennonite village founded without a single man in it. All the adults in it women, 147 of them, and her brother at fourteen the oldest male. Mostly they were widows. Some of them knew for certain, and others did not. Her mother never knew if her husband was shot the same night they took him away or if he was still felling trees in the gulag. So forty percent of the families they set down in the South American wilderness, she'd read in that book by Peter Dyck, were led by women alone, and there were thirty-two men whose wives were missing. And some of them, needing an extra hand and company, moved together, which wasn't in the rules. So the preachers said whoever lost their spouse because of the war and hadn't heard of their fate for seven years, was free to remarry. Seven years was a long time and no one had ever explained to her why that particular number.

So she'd gotten this far, with the history told as briefly as she could, hands sweeping the air, Russia up and Paraguay down and leftward over the ocean, Ava still following, it seemed. That's interesting, Oma, she said in between. Her mother's house at one end of the village and her sister's at the other, and every day she walked to her sister's place to assist her. She went in the morning and she stayed until noon. It was hotter and bleaker than anything they'd ever known. They made bricks. They plowed and planted. Her sister made a garden and she kept a cow.

And then one day, there he was. Johann. One of the precious so-called widowers, his wife and children like coins spilled through a hole in his pocket in an earlier life. He'd been riding down the street on a horse and seen her walking to her sister's and he said she was pretty. Like a filly, he said. He was thirty-three years to her seventeen, but he'd asked her mother permission to court her and Mama said, If you like her enough and if you treat her well, and then she'd asked her daughter, and she was willing too.

Mama also said, But you know he's been married before and has children, and she said, I think I like him and he's nearly free, isn't he, Mama? thinking of the seven-year rule, and Mama said, I mean in terms of his urgency, his experience. I wouldn't imagine he's waited six years, she said, and not had a friend or two, so can you forgive him, should it be so? And she had said, hearing but not understanding, Yes, I think I can. For he was a handsome man, and hard-working, but bold as well, and every woman in the village knew he'd come to court her and she'd felt their envy, like milk left in a pan. The sour taste of their questions, their remarks. He'd chosen her instead of one of them.

But who cared about them while he was speaking of her,

while he spoke of his longings and his past. He never pretended he hadn't had a wife and two sons. But she was young and lovely and strong, he said, and one evening when he was rich with his praises but sad as well, she took his hand and promised she would give him other sons, and maybe daughters too, and it seemed to comfort him, and the next day he helped them load their hay and he gave her mother farming advice, and at the end of the next week they celebrated their engagement on the yard with her sister and some neighbours, though not with a sermon as the custom was, because the preacher refused, the seven years not fully accomplished.

That evening, when the moon was high, he took her into the bush a way and showed her a queen of the night, the cactus flower he said would open only once, and only at night. He'd been keeping track. He wanted to surprise her. The flower seemed a flame, burning white in the moonlight. He had the horse with him, for returning to his village, so he put the saddle blanket on the ground and they lay on it and perhaps he was too experienced, as her mother had warned, and they began before they should have. The horse whinnied when they sat up and she told him it had hurt. He said, I'm sorry but it gets better, you know, and then he touched the wine-stain birthmark on her neck and said, I noticed this the first time I saw you but I've never noticed it since, except to think how beautiful it can be. He must have known she blushed, because she knew how it crept up her neck, like a spill with points over her jaw, her mother blaming it on some fright she'd had while pregnant. It resembles a J, he said, one side higher than the other, and you must think of me when you see it in a mirror, how I greet you with my love. He talked like that, in his moon-filled voice. And then they walked back to the yard and he was leading the horse and she went along with him as far as the gate to the street and there he kissed her again, distracted now, as if he no longer cared what her mother and all the women of the world might say, if they saw them.

He was like rainwater in that arid place, and if her mother seemed cross with her the next morning, what difference did it make? But the man who sat under the *algorrobo* tree with her next was the sallow preacher Goossen. He invited Mama to join them, but Mama said, If she's old enough to marry, she's old enough to hear this on her own. A clap of fear like thunder in her then, leaping in her birthmark, where she ached when she was nervous. And the long and the short of it was that Johann was gone, he'd left for the capital city that morning. He was on his way to Russia. Another refugee had told him his wife was alive and he knew where she was. Her heart a-jerk like it was dumped in a bag and shaken for fury and so the nearly seven years were null and void, and Johann with a dilemma he couldn't resolve, except like this. The preacher's voice too plump and gleaming with the burden of his news. He seemed to like his work of solace in the village of women, so many weak ones glad of a hand on their shoulder, an arm around their waist. Setting Johann in a noble light, as if she should bow before the saint and gladly let him go, for he'd done the right thing, hadn't he?

He went back to Russia then? Ava had cried, interrupting her, fingers anxious on the sugar spoon. She imagined he did, she answered, though there were rumours he'd travelled no farther than Argentina and found a German woman there, to have more sons with her. But who knew if it was true?

Her birthmark had throbbed while the preacher talked, but she gleaned what she could without revealing her concern, her sorrow. He wanted to fill the space under the tree with something besides her silence, it seemed, so he told her more and more. He said that Johann had known at their engagement, he'd found out while he was wooing her, and so the struggle had been terrible, and he'd confided in the preacher that he could not live a lie.

He would arrive in Russia in winter, she'd been thinking, such a pleasant change from the buzz of crickets and cicadas. But if a torture to be alone, as he'd said, it was a torture to her that he wouldn't have told her himself, and if courage to return, surely cowardice to run away without telling her the truth of it. That was the shame she had to get through from one end of the village to the other the very next day, when everyone already knew he'd chosen Siberia, and his gaunt and older wife instead of her. Picking up his rubbed-off rubles of a family. He could have kept his knowledge a secret, as others had. Some thought it served her right, so proud she'd been, holding her head that way, as if she were beautiful instead of marked with a double surge of red on her neck like a common harlot.

She doesn't know how much of this she said aloud to Ava, and how much was in her mind like a bath filling with bubbles. She tried to tell her as plainly as she could. She said her mother called off the wedding and she walked to her sister's with her neck long and straight as if she had a birthmark she wanted everyone to see.

And Ava, swift as a kick, as if playing some field game of hers, said, But Oma, *as if*? You *have* a mark, what do you mean, *as if*?

She did—she does—indeed, she said, and this was the point she wanted to reach. She was different because of the mark but she'd taught herself not to remember it. And those months she'd gone to help her sister, she'd not remembered it at all. She was tall and carefree, and she was envied instead. But that morning, after she'd been awake all night thinking of Johann in the capital, she couldn't forget no matter how much she tried. But she kept her head as high, just the same.

As if you know what you know, she said, in spite of what's true.

It sounded not quite logical as she said it and so she laughed, and Ava laughed and said, I know what you mean. Then Ava said she had to go, and no, she didn't want cookies or fudge along, she'd eaten far too much over Christmas. And off she went, her darling granddaughter, gay or whatever she is, ready for Toronto and her back straight, head up, and that little wave, like a salute. Into the elevator, and into the cold, the sun beginning its descent, gold on the rooftops, and in the shadows, a delicate blue.

Helping Isaak

PART ONE

I have only one sheet of paper from which to work. Bureaucratic stock, black ink on white, letters formed neatly, though paled by age, and aloof, it seems, as if displeased to be woken from sleep in these Soviet archives.

The narrative is brief, a slender archipelago of words. Each new line beyond the woman's name seems an afterthought.

January 6, 1930.
Margaret S., 27.
Of the German Mennonite sect.
Shot near B____.
On the river.
Pretending to play.
Fleeing to the other shore.

Children (2) apprehended.
Children returned.
Witnesses:
Local commander Vladimir K.,
Comrade Aron S. (husband and stepfather).
Her intention confirmed
(by the boy).

I will have to build backward from these words and admit, when I am finished, that I have built a house of straw. The fruitful steppe-like ground she fled, the winter days of vast bright sky, the summer days of rain, that beguiling horizon of mountains, even legends concerning cranes, can be discerned by common research. But what can soil and seasons tell me of this death?

And what does a river remember?

I stare at the page, as if awaiting further evidence. I find myself wondering who saw this piece of paper first, who filed it away.

One of those detestable GPU officers, I suppose, eager for fresh reports from the Amur Oblast. From the border communities. Forming his plans to scrape the river zone clean as if shaved, to empty it for a buffer of wooden watchtowers and military transport. A nice wide buffer for the wide Amur Dear Father, which the scheming Chinese on its nether bank called the Black Dragon.

Probably moving his lips, pinching them shut. A smile like a slash. Thinking, let's stop these escapes, these attempts, once and for all.

Was he curious about the game the woman and her children played? Which of the witnesses killed her?

Did he care what the boy may have said to give his mother's scheme away?

But this imagined official—this gloating, spying

bureaucrat—has nothing to do with my quest, nothing to do with helping Isaak. I must shake him away before he hardens in my mind.

I shake him away and then I write out the words of the report. One copy for me, and one for the old man Isaak.

PART TWO

There was so little to go on. I had the confirmation of her death; those several details. They seemed inadequate for the sadness I remembered in his face, in his hands, when he pressed money upon me, asking me—since I conducted my research in the places he had lived—if I might look for this case.

I found the document, and then a story formed. It formed in spite of my professional training, in spite of my professional intentions. It filled the missing spaces, as stories will, and when I came back, when I handed him the report I'd copied, I sat down beside him and spoke as long and as liltingly as I could about what I'd found and what I imagined. I leaned toward him and spoke to him as if he were a child once more, this old bent man, the hair as sparse as it may have been when he was an infant, as if he were wrapped to suckle, to learn the sound of a mother's cooing voice. He seemed willing to listen and this—more or less—is the story I told him:

I see Margaret in the garden, I said, the summer before the report of her death, on the morning Aron asked her to marry him. She is squatting to the potato plants, hoe crooked into her arm and leaning against her. She is lifting their leaves, plucking at the weeds.

She positions herself so Isaak, who is five and malnourished, is always in view. Today he helps his sister carry wood. Margaret registers their intermittent steps, their scampers, as strain within her back, as if her body is the earth they walk upon, six-year-old Lensch with her bossy, confident manner and the boy, proud of his ability to help but also bewildered—or so it seems to his mother—at the weight of his participation.

Not the weight of the wood but the solemnity that surrounds it: why the pieces have to be set down so precisely by the door, why he and his sister have to stay outside until noon, why inside and outside are categories on this yard instead of one whole thing as when his father was alive—not that the boy remembers how things once were, though he claims he remembers his father. His big strong Papa. Lensch declares she remembers her father too. She instructs her brother as if it's true but she's simply aping what Margaret has taught them both.

Aron emerges from the barn. His gait is nervous and determined. He has forced himself out to do what he has decided to do. To do what Margaret wants, and doesn't want, her wishes tangling like the detritus the river abandoned when it flooded its banks last spring. She doesn't have the leisure, the calmness of mind, to sort through them for what the answer should be. Just to know the proposal is coming seems useful enough for now, gives her another angle to consider besides the one she is forming with Vladimir when she does his housework at his residence in the village near the river, because she needs the money.

She stands up, takes a step, squats again. Aron tousles Isaak's head as he passes him and Margaret hears the child's squeal, as if happy or hurt. A blessing it's hot, she thinks; the children's clothes are threadbare. For some months now it won't matter, not the way it matters in the winter. Crossing in summer requires one set of plans, winter another. In summer she will need a boat. In winter the Amur freezes. She hasn't decided yet for which time of the year she should aim.

Aron reaches Margaret and he stops. The pale short shadow his body makes at this time of the day drops into the garden row between them.

"Margaret," he says, speaking her name whole instead of "Greta" as usual. "Let me see the hoe."

Margaret is nervous too, shaking like a schoolgirl about to recite at the Christmas program, every eye upon her a prediction of failure. She gets up slowly, as smoothly as she can. She remembers shinnying up the apple tree in her father's orchard when she was young, consumed with anticipation of blue sky or white cloud beyond the thick foliage of her upward journey. Now she gains, as she moves, Aron's worn boots and then his legs, his waist and chest, his arms, his neck, and there he is, revealed to her against the warm summer sky. It surprises her that she is happy to reach him.

She is much shorter than he is; a disadvantage. She steps back, to make the angle of her tilted face more appealing. They may be impoverished but she has beauty to spend.

"Aron," she replies.

He has not come about the hoe but he takes it from her, upends it, asks, "Is it sharp enough?"

Margaret says, "It seems fine," then adds, "Do you think it will rain?"

"It's the season," he says. The sky is cloudless.

They enact this charade, she thinks, for his mother, who may have glimpsed them through the window, who may burst through the door of their shed-house here at the farthest end of the Soviet Union at any moment now, calling "Aron? Aron?" As if she passes her days in a fog and needs to take constant soundings of where he is, to be reassured that, after losing one son to typhus, the other is still alive.

But Margaret is dazzled by his height, as if she was tricked, as if she had forgotten that Aron is no longer the thirteen-year-old he was when she married his brother. That he is broader, and handsome, and dangerous.

Then he says, "I know I'm six years younger than you are. I'm a year older than you were when you married my brother. He was twenty then, I'm twenty now. You need a husband, the children need a father. I'm ready to marry. I could marry you."

Margaret smiles at his logic and he stiffens.

"You're laughing," he says.

"Oh no," she says. She knows how systematic Aron is, how often he rearranges his possessions in the rough wooden box he keeps beside his bed. "Perhaps I noticed something already."

Aron is assessing her. His eyes are nearly black and Margaret feels transparent in front of them, like a shard of ice, dissolving. Her worries may be visible too—what to do about him and Vladimir and the children, and how she will manage the promise she made to her late husband Franz.

"What's there been to notice?" he asks. "What have I done? What have I said?"

Margaret's curly hair is braided, wound up, tucked under a kerchief, but strands of it have escaped to her forehead. She brushes them back, shifts closer to him.

"A woman senses things," she says. "Nothing obvious to anyone else, I'm sure." Though she is certain his mother and his sister, maybe even his father, have guessed at his interest. They notice far more about her than they should, and their notice has taken on envy like moisture in a sack of beans, swelling and spoiling what they see. They don't like her as much as they did before she was widowed and cast on their meagre resources; she and the children, three mouths to feed.

Aron says, "I suppose you're good at sensing then." He shrugs, as if to cast her powers aside, but seems unsure of himself and becomes rigid again.

He's taller than Franz was, than Vladimir is, and big-boned, but enough like Margaret's dead husband at this proximity to confuse her, especially after he's asked her to marry him. The memory of her late husband's body seems to lurk inside the young man's clothes, and Margaret suddenly realizes, fearful of its portent, that Aron's shirt was Franz's once, and then the fear gives way to yearning and she's shaking again. She knows the parts of a man that she was ignorant of the first time she married and she wishes Aron would give her the hoe. The fledgling potato plants are drowning in weeds.

His mouth resembles Franz's too. She must not look; she will stare at his throat instead where the skin is ruddy and taut. But perhaps it is soft. She wishes she could touch it to know one way or the other, to test her strength, to warn him perhaps. Aron is dangerous, and not just because of the rumours that he's sympathetic to the police, the communist organizers, the border guards. To authorities in whatever form they take. An informer. It can't be proved, of course, because they all display sympathies of various kinds; they all act in ways diametrically opposed to their thinking; all of them try to keep on good terms with everyone they meet. They jostle for safety, for possible advantage.

But she watched him kill a dog in his rage. She, searching for dill around the back of the summerhouse, and Aron, supposing himself alone, clubbing the dog to death. The post upon the canine's head so accurate the animal crumpled immediately, Aron dropping then, chest down and over, muffling the first and only yowl, a wisp of sound escaping like an airborne seed, insubstantial and unlikely to excite anyone's attention. And if she hoped his dropping was regret, she was disappointed, for he

got up and brushed the front of his tunic, dragged the beast to
looser ground, dug a shallow hole, and he whistled all the while.
And she, pressed into the doorway of the summerhouse, unable
to move lest she startle and enrage him again.

Aron was sixteen then, when she and Franz lived in
Slavgorod, in the parents' summerhouse. He said that the dog
must have run away or been stolen, and Margaret kept quiet
because Franz was fond of his younger brother.

"So," he is asking her now, "what do you say?"

"Ah!" Margaret gasps. She hears a solitary sound, a hint of a
horn-like call, high and far away.

Cranes.

Surely impossible. Not now. And then she sighs, as if to
answer with a prayer, *Oh that I had wings, to fly away and rest.*
Her husband Franz had been the village teacher. They were
poor, but he'd gathered knowledge of cranes. Large birds, he
murmured in her ear as they lay close in bed. And vocal. Birds
of legend, the signs of good fortune. Of a long life. He nuzzled
her, divulged his information as an invitation. If you meet a
crane, he said, your difficulties end, your hard life is over. And
when they mate, they dance, he said. They lift their heads to the
heavens and call in unison, for joy.

She may be mistaken about what she heard, but it's because
of the crane-sound, real or imagined, that she is stammering
now. His proposal, she says, has caught her unprepared.

He says, "You said you weren't surprised."

She shakes her head, reminds herself to concentrate. "Not
surprised. But should I have decided before I knew for certain
you would ask?" Lensch is heading their way and Margaret
motions for a break in the conversation.

Aron rights the hoe, stabs at a clump of dirt.

"I'm busy with the garden, Lensch," Margaret calls. Anx-
iously, as if gardening brings her into peril. "Leave your chores

for now, run—you and your brother. Run down the lane! A little game with him!"

Lensch glances from her mother to Aron and back again, her expression unhappy, but she nods. She returns to her brother.

They collaborate, Margaret thinks, she and Lensch, raising the boy. It's little Isaak they have to pull through. He's too thin, too sensitive; he tries too hard to be good, to understand. It will only burden him.

"You need a father for the children," Aron mutters. It seems a complaint.

"And how do we live as husband and wife?" Margaret complains in return. "All of us in one room. Your parents and sister too."

"Why wouldn't we get a little house of our own?"

"Yes, of course, but that's difficult now, isn't it? I mean…" They are sparring already; speaking out space to maneuvre. This marrying will not be for love, she thinks, if it happens at all.

Still, she asks. "Do you love me?"

Aron flushes.

"I don't need a husband offered out of duty," she says.

"Oh Greta," Aron groans. "You have no idea!"

His words seem an ache that has surfaced as a wound and the difference in their ages looms. Now Margaret knows for sure that he's deeply sunk with his fantasies of union, with his dreams of her body, his needs.

It may be a help to her.

Aron steps back. "I wouldn't have asked," he says formally, "without both. Duty *and* love."

Margaret slows her breath. "Well answered," she says.

"But have you answered *me*? Shall I beg to also know if you love me, without knowing whether you'll accept my proposal? And could I suppose the one from the other?"

Ah, Aron. Clever, charming Aron.

The children have begun to squabble. Isaak runs, trips, and falls. Lensch helps him up and he begins to cry. Aron's sister Elsa is standing on the stoop. She peers at Aron and Margaret. She scowls.

Margaret speaks in a rush, says there's so much to think of, she must have a month.

Aron releases the hoe. The handle falls forward and nearly hits her foot but Margaret doesn't move.

"I'll speak to you in a month," he says.

He turns, but so quickly that she cannot tell if he turned with hope or displeasure. He strides away.

"Coming," Margaret calls to the children, her voice low, apologetic. Her heart clatters with fear. She has been scheming, night after night, how they will leave. It's all she wants. Just to escape, as some others have escaped over the river, word trickling back that they reached Harbin in China, where they expect doors will open to America, where they expect to be free. It was her husband's wish. Franz would understand that whatever she does, whomever she marries or kisses, it is only because he asked her to flee.

Part Three

Old Isaak listens to what I say and then he starts his ramblings again, from the beginning, everything he told me the first time, when he made his request. As if we're strangers and have just met.

Before he dies, he tells me, he wants the consolation of knowledge. His sister Lensch is dead but she had told him everything she knew. He could circle his maypole of endless speculation if he wanted to, she said, but she would not dance. Lensch was not an optimistic person, Isaak says, but she possessed more endurance than anyone he knew and his constant wavering unnerved her. The problem was, her memories seemed so sure and he had next to none at all. He had the facts—his mother Margaret gone, his stepfather Aron soon gone too—and vague impressions like dreams that leave nothing but their aura behind. His mother had married his uncle, that much he knew, and sometimes she worked as a housekeeper in the homes of officials, of the military police, somewhere close to the river. He usually went along with her.

His mother talked with one man in particular—perhaps this Vladimir on the document I found and copied—and the conversations were animated, pitched high, exclusive, but he admits he may have been jealous of her attentions. Sometimes the man ordered him outside to play alone. He recalls being cold and miserable, his cheek pressed to the door.

Isaak says there are people who spend their lives investigating mysteries of science or philosophy. They discover some problem that no one has solved. They cannot be satisfied to leave it alone. It's a summons, he says, like a vocation—to think upon, to examine every side of the unresolved matter that possesses them. They're patient and persistent, he says, for they believe the solution is already there, even while it remains undiscovered. They believe this because the answer is the source, the origin, of their call.

In his case, Isaak goes on, the mystery has been personal, and though it's large to him, it is of no consequence to anyone else. It has not preoccupied him in equal measure throughout his life, but neither has he ever lived entirely free of the question of what happened to his mother.

Because of this, he says, as if he's now remembered who I am, he appreciates that his bit of money made it possible for me to find the report of her case. Now, he says, he can know for certain that she had not abandoned them. That she was killed.

Perhaps he has always known this, he says, but he never saw her bloody body in the snow as his sister claimed she had. He may have fallen. He may have been carried away. He remembers a man on a horse and leafless willows bending toward him on the riverbank.

And yes, the two names on the report: Aron, his stepfather, and Vladimir, the local commander. Isaak realizes, he says, that absolute clarity will probably not be possible on the roles they played. On who surprised whom. As the paper says, both of them were there. His stepfather was taken to an asylum, where he died or was murdered. Their Aunt Elsa cared for him and Lensch. She'd been greedy for children, she told them later, but the apple she'd longed for was sour when she ate it.

As for my story, Isaak seems amused by the frank way I've imagined his mother. And his vulnerability as a child. It's certainly plausible, he says; it makes no difference now. When he asks me if the report contained any mention of him, any problem he may have caused for his mother's plan to cross the Amur, I point at the words on his copy of the document, on which I deleted the last two lines. No, I say, as firmly as I can.

"Look," I say. "There's no such thing."

He pauses, as if to consider this. Then he says he's glad I thought of the cranes. He never told Lensch, he says, but he might as well tell me. He encountered a crane, a red-crowned crane, near a marsh he wandered to in the lost months after his mother was gone and his sister was put to work in the kitchen and no one seemed to be minding him. It was just before he and Lensch, together with his aunt and their grandparents, were removed to central Siberia. He spent the rest of his life in Siberia, he reminds me, until many years later when things changed in the Soviet Union and he, now a widower, emigrated west with his grown children, to Germany.

The crane was alone. It looked at him and he looked back. It may have given him longevity, he says, but it never brought him good fortune.

When he asked about or lamented their mother, Lensch would say, "The angels came and they took her away." She said angels but he imagined them cranes, necks outstretched and honking as they swooped to pick his mother up. Throughout his boyhood, he says, he interchanged angels and cranes.

He tells me that when he was grown and his sister refused to discuss the past any further, he built a small refuge in his heart, a small resistant closed box of his own where he kept his unresolved questions. Inside that box, he says, the crane he had seen in the marsh was his mother. *Margaret S., 27.* He remembered that she turned southwards as she rose and, flying ever higher until she couldn't be seen, she must have crossed the river. The border between Russia and China.

Then Isaak assumes the overly cheerful expression the hard of hearing sometimes put on when it's too much work to continue a conversation. He touches my hand briefly as if to pity— or forgive—me. He tries to straighten his back away from me, and his head bends and his eyes close.

He's ready for a nap, I suppose. I watch as he drifts away, his body slackening and the smile loosening too, until there's just the tiniest curve of it left. He's finished with me but I watch him for a while. I imagine him refolding what he knows, and what he doesn't, sliding it inside the worn envelope of his longing. I hope he's comforted, and not disappointed.

Being Here

After church, the light is intense and it's hot. Liese puts on her sunglasses before she sets out across the parking lot. The car is at the far end. They were late again and there were no spots closer. But she likes walking through the strong warmth of the day. It reminds her of walking into the water at the lake, the waves surging around her.

She feels heat rising off the asphalt too, along her legs, through her sandals. She wonders if pavement enjoys the sun on its back. It's because they had their driveway paved, just a month ago, and she'd sat on the front porch with her coffee, watching the pair of men spreading the heavy black mixture as it slid from the chute, and she'd stayed out there even when one of them grumbled loud enough for her to hear, "Lady, we know what we're doing, you don't have to keep an eye on us!" She'd stayed there, sipping at her empty cup, and called back in a deliberate, cheerful voice, "I'm not checking up on you. I'm interested in the process!"

The other man, who seemed younger, had straightened and

stopped his work to say, pointing at his partner, "Frank gets nervous 'round the women." He'd shrugged and grinned.

She'd been pondering the ideal—the essential—state of being asphalt. Was it boiling tar and gravel? Cooling and hardening would be a terrible letdown then, and any kind of warmth a pleasant memory. Was it a smooth hard finish? Then cooling would be a triumph and the prior heat a test, a kind of suffering.

She'd caught herself playing with these questions—how peculiar the thoughts that came to her sometimes!—and felt embarrassed, as if they were visible and the men would see how strange and ignorant she was. She'd left the porch abruptly, for this reason and not to spare poor nervous Frank.

And now she's remembering that she'd asked her parents, when she was a girl, how old people were in the afterlife. Did it have to be the age at which they died or could they choose their best—their favourite—time? Her mother had snapped at her, "The things you come up with!" but her father replied, as if he didn't find her impertinent, "Well, Liese, I've thought of that myself."

Mama had been frying chicken and the hot fat sizzled behind his words. "On the river that winter," he said, "on the Amur, when I feared I wouldn't reach the shore because my feet were freezing and I'd lost my way, I remember thinking I wanted to be older than this after my death. I felt too young. I felt too empty."

He'd paused and said, "We'll have to see, I guess. God knows."

God knows. This was the answer for everything her parents didn't know. It's probably the answer for the perfect state of being asphalt too. But it vexes her sometimes, that she has only one life in which to spend her experiences. She goes through them in such a muddle half the time, not knowing when she's happiest, whether it's a condition that's past or still ahead of her.

She's reached the car and sees Johnnie and Michael inside it already, waiting for her. They've got the engine running, the air conditioning on maximum. They're cooling off. She reaches for the door handle, and then she hears her name.

Gloria Harder is hurrying toward her. When she gets close enough, she tells Liese that she likes her hair.

Liese lifts her hand from the car and touches a strand of hair by her ear. "Thanks," she says. "Thanks." She had it trimmed and layered this week, the grey covered.

Gloria Harder is the head of the women's ministries at church, and now she's head of the new refugee committee as well. She reported about that in the morning's service. She's asking Liese to come share a little something at the next women's meeting. She knows Liese works shifts at the store but she hopes she can arrange to be free that evening. She says the women need to hear a little something about what it's like to be an immigrant.

It's getting too hot to be standing in the sun, no shade on the lot, but Gloria's voice is breezy and her repetition of *a little something* sounds cool and comfortable. Liese admires and resents Gloria in equal measure, though she's been trying to pitch her attitude, generally, in the direction of admiration. It's not that easy, she's finding, and coming back to church hasn't made it easier either.

Liese has seniority at the store and works only days by now, so the evening won't be a problem, but she doesn't tell Gloria this. She's taken aback at the request, as if she brought it on herself by recalling that conversation with her parents, who stayed behind in Paraguay while she came to Canada.

"I don't think of myself as an immigrant," she says. "I've been here more than thirty years."

Gloria is wearing a sleeveless, sand-coloured dress that's crisp and cottony, and ringing her throat is a necklace made of tiny shells, painted turquoise and glazed to a high sheen. Safe behind her dark glasses, Liese memorizes the combination. Informal, yet elegant too. The colours like ads you see for the

Caribbean. She would be attracted to a necklace like that, hold it up against herself. Maybe even buy it. Then never wear it. Shells on a string! Not to church at least.

She'd meant *immigrant* in a technical sense, Gloria says. She didn't think of Liese that way either. "Still," she says, "thirty years is a lot of practice. There's so much you can teach us, that's the point, and if we're going to get this refugee sponsorship right, we'll need to understand how it feels on the other side." They'd thought of her immediately, she says.

"You seem so beautifully adjusted," Gloria goes on in her smooth, tanning-lotion voice. "I'd quite forgotten that you came from Paraguay once, I really had, but someone on the committee remembered, and it seemed obvious, you must have a wealth of wisdom to share. Of how one adjusts and everything."

Thought of her immediately?

Gloria is suggesting that Liese make a list. Five, six, seven, maybe ten pieces of advice. Or tell some stories. The funny things that happened.

"I remember this woman from Paraguay who cleaned for me," Gloria says. "I've forgotten her name because eventually I got someone else—she wasn't quite finicky enough for my tastes, though people always say, get the Mennonite women from Paraguay, they know how to work, so that's what I look for. Anyway, she told me this story about her first winter, how she bought boots but they were rubber boots, for rain, and of course she went flying on the first patch of ice in winter and they weren't warm either and—" Gloria laughs, the sound of it as bright as her blue, varnished shells.

Is it help they want, or a circus act? Liese feels the acid of her thoughts, though she hasn't stopped smiling. She senses son Michael glaring at her from the back seat of the car. He's hungry, of course, and wants to get home.

"I'm no good at public speaking," she says.

"Oh, my goodness, it's not a speech! Just come and share yourself with us. Just a little something of yourself."

Liese swallows. How hard she's tried, how unsuccessfully, to become the kind of bread she can break off and share with others.

"Pray about it," Gloria says. "I'm sure the Lord will give you the words."

"I know." Liese turns slightly, toward the car. "Sorry, Gloria, but these guys are famished. I have to go. I'll think about it. I'll let you know." She opens the car door.

"I wasn't a refugee though," she says. "Refugee might be different than immigrant."

"Yes, yes, of course. But being here! That's the thing."

"I'll think about it."

"Great!" Gloria says, lifting her hand as if to bless Liese or wave. "I'll call you Tuesday. I really really hope you do! You'd be terrific."

Liese tells Johnnie what Gloria wanted. "That sounds good," he says.

"I told her I'd think about it. I didn't want to give her a chance to ask if I clean houses on the side."

Liese hears her husband clear his throat, as if to find a pitch to match the hum of the air conditioning. She recognizes the rebuke in it. Don't be so critical, he's trying to say, don't be so sensitive.

"I told her I'd think about it," she repeats.

She thinks about it. She tries to come up with a little something—a list of little somethings—for the church women who are eager to get into refugee work. Four times Liese tries, beginning on Sunday afternoon while Johnnie snoozes in front of the television, and then again that evening, and twice on Monday.

She sits at the table with a piece of paper.

On her first attempt, she sets down the numbers from one to five.

She writes *Everything is new* beside the number one.

Beside the two, she puts *It's sometimes hard.*

At the three, *But it's good, if you have a good enough reason to be here.*

This is not advice; it's stating the obvious. It's not stories. Not jokes. She's too serious for jokes. She only laughs with Johnnie, and it's his jokes, his teasing, that sets her off. She laughs to affirm that she loves him. A kind of recommitment. But she's not funny herself.

Liese tears the paper into pieces.

On her second attempt, she starts on a clean sheet with the numbers one to six. She stares at the lines, can't think of a thing, and the page stays blank.

On Monday, she adds seven to ten to the numbers one to six.

She has stories, of course she does. They're gathering in her mind. But she's not used to thinking of them as fables, as lessons for others.

Towels, she thinks. They ought to be new. No refugee or immigrant wants used towels, thin and fraying. She imagines herself lecturing the women, her nails fire red and her pointer finger aimed at their heads. "Think, people, think. Our skin collects water the way yours does. If a towel's no longer absorbent enough for your dear bottoms, it's not absorbent enough for ours."

Liese sighs. This is too specific. And too bitter, of course. The poor refugee family their church is sponsoring will be inundated with towels.

She remembers the line from the Leonard Cohen song. Maybe that's a way to begin. *And everyone to love will come...* She writes it down as number one.

Number two: *but as a refugee.* Nice touch, indeed.

But it's nonsense. It sounds like a sermon, and she wasn't asked to preach.

She can't do it. She won't. She has stories, yes, but fewer than expected and they're not useful at all. She knows what Gloria and the other women want. They'll want her to go on and on about how wonderful Canada is, how wonderful wonderful wonderful, like a campfire ditty. As if she's under obligation to spend her life praising this place, just because they let her stay. Hasn't she been here long enough to complain like those born here?

Of course she loves it, but one place is as good or as awful as another. She won't give them gush, she thinks, and she won't give them grumble.

But her very knowledge has marked her. Immigrant inside and out. Knowledge that feels like shame. Resentment. About the need to praise, to mollify forever-residents as if she's their captive and working for release. She's long past her insecurities. Or is she? There's any number of lines that still waver for her between gaudy or sophisticated, lines that seem clear for women like Gloria with their sleeveless sand-coloured cotton dresses and turquoise shell necklaces. Arms browned to just the right depth of contrast.

Her freckles probably rose to the surface of her face and arms while she and Gloria talked in the sun, born as she was in the green hell of the Paraguayan Chaco, the sun her fate, and Gloria squinting unafraid against the light, running a hand through her bangs, saying apologetically, "My roots are showing." But Gloria didn't care about her roots. Or Liese's hair either. It was just about getting Liese to come talk to their women about being an immigrant. Being here, from there.

"Just those adjustments, those feelings," she'd said.

Liese's stories, too unwieldy to tell, lean against each other like objects thrown into a box for the thrift store. Crazy wishes and joys and, yes, adjustments.

The heat persists through Monday and into Tuesday. Everyone in the city is waiting for it to break, waiting for a cooling rain. One waits a long while, sometimes, even suffers a little, for those sweet moments of release, something close to perfection.

When Gloria calls on Tuesday afternoon, Liese says no, she'd really rather not, and her stomach tightens, anticipating Gloria's disappointment, and maybe God's too. But the fear passes, and when the conversation ends, more friendly than it might have been under the circumstances, Liese feels fine again, happy and herself, as if the prayer she'd been afraid to utter has, in fact, been answered.

White

She's ten years old and hiding in a thicket of mulberry bushes, spying on the children of the English-speaking family next door. It's not the first time. She's been watching them on and off since they arrived in the colony centre a week ago.

Liese is new to Filadelfia too, but she hasn't come from far away. She's always lived in the Paraguayan Chaco, in the Mennonite settlement. She's never been anywhere else. Her father got a job in the peanut processing plant, so they left their farm in the village and moved into town. She'll miss her village friends but she knows the town is more important. The presence of these foreigners confirms it.

There are two boys and a girl. She thinks they're younger than she is, though the oldest—a boy—may be close to her age. He bosses the play. Today the three of them burst from their house with an assortment of dolls and cars and trucks, which they've arranged on the yard. Each has a territory of their own, it seems, though they meet at sites common to all. The girl takes care of the dolls and the boys manage the vehicles.

The children rove heedlessly between the sun and the shade, as if oblivious to the difference between them, and Liese nearly calls, "Stay out of the boiling sun," as her mother does during the hottest season of the year—just beginning now, in November, the summer holiday—but then she remembers that this will give her away. And the children won't understand her German. But perhaps their skin won't burn as hers—pale and freckled—does. Their hair is dark and hers is blonde, heavily tinged with red.

Liese knows the children come from America. The adults around her speak often of America, or Canada, which are found—as it's been explained to her—on the top half of the earth ball, where Russia also lies, though further around it, over the ocean. Canada and America seem overlapping places to her, full of Mennonites too, but luckier and richer ones who are cheerful when they visit the Chaco, though their faces sometimes glimmer with astonishment she can't quite trust. She fears they're as pessimistic as the Mennonites who live here are about their prospects in this hot and difficult place.

Her father says their neighbours moved to Paraguay so the man can help the farmers with their problems concerning cattle and crops. Liese assumes that when the problems are solved, the family will leave and return to their home. She expects it won't be long for, coming from America, the man will have many answers already.

So she's watching the children now, with some urgency. And her mouth may be open. "Close your mouth," her oldest sister Tina, impatient as a broom, will often hiss at her, even when she's sure it is closed. But she's mesmerized by the strange sounds of the children playing in English, comprehensible to one another, amiable too it seems, but a great provocation to her, like a shrieking tree-full of wild parrots.

Then the children's voices grow angry and there's a skirmish over one of the boxes. The girl breaks away and dashes to the house, yelling "Mom-my! Mom-my!" as if injured. At the door, the children's mother steps out to meet her. Liese decides *Mommy* is the English word for *Mama.*

How clever she feels at that moment, deciphering a piece of their speech! But hard on the back of her pleasure, like an unexpected shiver in the heat, is her consciousness of being alone, and hidden, as uneasy as a secret. She feels that she's loosely constructed and vulnerable, like a spider's web, instead of real and substantial as the American children are. Her desire to know them increases; it swells as she sees them disappear into the house behind their mother, minus the scattered objects of their make-believe habitation—the dolls and cars and trucks. Liese wants their toys, their language, their strangeness, their confidence. She heard the mother soothe the girl and then the boys who shuffled near, heads down and anxious, and she wants the consolation they're given and their bravery and humility. She wants everything about them.

Liese studies the American family as much as she can, whenever her mother or Tina haven't discovered a chore for her to do. She stares from the verandah, or from her perch in the mulberry hedge. She sees that the children's mother, while at home, wears pretty dresses with narrow waists and full skirts, but dressing up—for the store, or a meeting perhaps—she puts on one of two sleek outfits with narrow skirts and straight lines, the one a light brown colour like the soil of their garden but clean-looking, the other a dark blue, almost grey, like storm clouds with the hope of rain.

On her dressed-up occasions the woman's face is bright and her lips are redder than the lips of every other woman Liese knows. She feels this is probably the sheen of worldliness against which the preachers warn and it troubles her on behalf of the children's mother, because she's beautiful and seems so kind. Even spotting the foreign family in the town's church on Sunday doesn't alleviate her apprehension.

After the service, she approaches her father under the *algor-robo* tree. He's peeling a grapefruit with his pocketknife, cutting it away in one continuous strip that drops into a tangle of white and yellow on the packed earth at his feet.

Liese picks up the end of the peel and the coil falls opens and tears in half. "Papa," she says, "will the American lady beside us go to heaven? I think she wears lipstick."

Her father tugs off a segment of the grapefruit. "Why not?" he says.

Why not? Startling—and room to maneuvre, then. She won't probe further lest he made a mistake; she won't squander its possibilities. She drops to the ground beside her father's low three-legged stool, takes the grapefruit wedges he offers her, slurps their sweet juiciness.

This, she'll recollect many years later, is when her dream to move away from the Chaco began. As far as she's concerned, it was her father who gave her permission to be someone else.

Liese hung on to the dream of leaving long after the English-speaking family went back to their country. She hung on in spite of Mama's resistance every time she mentioned it. After high school, she worked in the local Co-op. Bored, she went to Asuncion, the capital, to make up beds and clean rooms in a German *pension*. She kept mentioning the matter of leaving. But perhaps it was simply habit by then, for she did nothing about it.

Still, her mother's misery over the very idea intensified. Mama wasn't that fond of the primitive, dusty Chaco herself—she'd admitted as much—but her loyalty had grown fierce over the years, her stories of hardships endured on its behalf irrefutable. And achieved, it seemed, through a dogged submission to Liese's father, who believed it was God and not the Mennonite Central Committee who had brought them to Paraguay. Mama sometimes cried in the middle of their arguments. She acted as if Liese's desire to leave was a criticism directed at her.

Then she got it into her head that Liese was attached to Alberto, a Paraguayan of the Spanish-speaking—not Mennonite—variety, whose name had come up in Liese's letters from Asuncion. Attached and likely to marry him. She panicked.

"I was thinking," her mother wrote, "why don't you go to Canada? Just for a while perhaps? Stay with the cousins. You need a change."

Liese understood the reason for her mother's reversal and said it was ridiculous. Couldn't a person stroll around the city with a friend without planning to marry him?

"You have no idea about Paraguayan men," Mama retorted by return mail.

Her letters pleaded and they pushed. They arrived in the capital like volleys, and then one day the source of them, Mama herself, was at Liese's *pension* door.

"All your life you talk big about leaving," she said. "Now I agree with you, so you better get going. Go for a visit at least. I've written the cousins." She took Liese to MennoTour for her papers and tickets; she and Papa, she said, would pay for everything.

Mama's unexpected arrival disarmed Liese. It stirred up her love for her mother and it stirred up her dream. Mama was right, of course. It's what Liese had wanted for years, and she wanted it still.

So she left her homeland. It was 1972, and she was twenty-one.

When she thinks about it, these many years later—her journey to Canada, her arrival—she remembers white. That continuous vista of clouds beneath the airplane. Thick, sun-catching cumulus, as if the entire cotton harvest of Paraguay had been spilled in farewell. Not straight off the field, but washed and dried, all the seeds and grime picked out of it.

And the cousins' small white house, and how she wondered, when they first stopped in front of it, whether it was freshly painted, just for her. Wondered, but didn't ask. Had never asked.

And the ironed white sheets of her bed in their basement, like an envelope she slipped into, exhausted, and slept in soundly until late the next morning. Until noon.

She has come to associate white with a kind of happiness—even, perhaps, with perfect peace. The sense of infinite potential, for example, that fog suggests, pressing its pearly bulk against the kitchen window, wrapping the yard away from her and breathing quietly, closely, until the sun dissolves it. Or the radiance of the bedroom some Saturday mornings when she sits in bed in her bathrobe, reading, the daylight filtered through the white sheers of the window, the outside world a blur through that veil and the inside sweet with silence, with time alone for a book or the newspaper, Johnnie out for breakfast or golf with his friends, when it seems that the past and the future can be grasped as a whole, the way one's whole life can be grasped, they say, just before drowning or dying in an accident. Simply seeing it and knowing without fear that it's fine; it's okay.

On the flight from Toronto, where she'd landed from Asuncion via Buenos Aires, she had the seat by the window. A woman travelling with a toddler was seated next to her. The child was restless. She clambered over Liese with her sharp bony elbows and knees to press her nose against the window. She saw the clouds and squealed, "Mommy, Mommy!"

It seemed a good omen, something of no consequence that

felt remarkable too: her first English word—"Mommy!"—reappearing on her way to Canada like the end mark of a parenthesis opened more than a decade ago. She said "No speak English" to the woman, and grinned at the girl, grinned at her until her jaw ached, while the child crawled back and forth over her lap, saying the one word she already knew.

Neither Liese nor her parents had ever seen Mama's cousins Nettie and Alvina, who lived in Winnipeg. They had a photograph, though, a studio portrait of them together. They were wearing white blouses with collars of crocheted lace, their partial smiles nearly identical. They seemed old to Liese, and she said so, but Mama told her they weren't that old at all; she believed they were only a few years older than she was. Late fifties, early sixties perhaps.

They were the daughters of Mama's eldest brother who fled Russia much earlier than Liese's parents had, who managed to get into Canada, where he found a wife. Both he and the wife were dead now, but they'd had these two, this Nettie and Alvina. One of them, Mama said, was single and the other had married, only to have her husband die of a stroke half a year later. The short-lived bride moved back home to her sister and they'd lived together ever since, in the house where they grew up.

Liese picked out the cousins in the Winnipeg terminal immediately but then she couldn't recall which name went with which woman. She must have been anticipating them as one, Nettie and Alvina, linked without further thought like the singsong syllables of a nursery rhyme. They introduced themselves but the arrivals area was noisy and she was distracted by the smell of hair-perming solution that lifted from their tightly curled, greyish-brown hair as they embraced her. Altogether, it was awkward, those first greetings, those first hurried mutual appraisals.

She was alert for grief on one of their faces and they, she felt, were surprised at her—that she was so modern-looking per-haps? Her hair was long and straight and parted in the middle, and she had clunky shoes and a short skirt in seventies fashion, though her skirt wasn't nearly as short as it would be soon, after she re-hemmed it in the privacy of her basement room, far from Mama's piercing disapproval.

Her cousins spoke German to her but Liese noticed it had suffered; it was thoroughly infected with English. She was pleased. She felt herself leaning toward their clumsy cadences as if linguistic loss might be contagious. Liese planned to be fluent in English in no time at all.

She was mortified, though, not knowing their names, not recalling enough about them to keep them apart. She would owe the cousins a huge debt of gratitude, Mama had said, for letting her live with them, and now this predicament, this stupidity. It seemed a first instance of what being here could entail: endless obligations she would fail at but could never forget.

But the cousins seemed warm and genuinely glad to see her, even deferential. They took turns telling her things or asking her questions about her trip and her parents in Paraguay until they left the building and packed her two bags in the trunk of their tan-coloured car. Then both of them—Nettie and Alvina, driver and passenger, whoever was which—concentrated on the road and Liese was left to her first impressions of Winnipeg, a city surprisingly calm and empty-looking, full of trees and lawns in an unassuming, dignified green, not the lush and steamy green of Asuncion, a city that seemed inferior already, and where, con-trary to what she'd claimed to her mother, she *had* been falling for Alberto, simply because, once again, she was bored. He'd professed undying love for her the night before she left, trying to kiss her at the gate of the Menno Heim, but she'd laughed and pulled away. She didn't believe his avowals but she no longer needed to hear them either.

They turned into the driveway of a square white house, its foundation rimmed with a profusion of flowers of various heights in yellow, blue, pink, and red. It seemed too sentimental, too disorganized, for Liese's vision of Canada; it was the kind of flower bed her mother would favour. Still, she had to admit it was cheerful and open-hearted and surely boded well for the work that lay before her, of becoming herself.

One sister said to the other, opening the trunk, "Well Nettie, why don't you take Liese down to her room?"

This time Liese paid attention. The woman who led her down the stairs had a mole on the far edge of her jaw so Nettie, she told herself, was the sister with the mole. Nettie took her into a tiny room at the far end of the basement. She showed her the bed, the narrow closet, the three-drawer dresser. She pointed to the empty wooden hangers on the closet rod. Then she was still for a moment, as if considering what else could be shown.

"Ah!" she said, opening the top dresser drawer. They'd collected some things for her, she said: small samples of soap and shampoo and flat perfume strips inside thin cellophane wrappers. She explained that the perfume packets sometimes came along with bills from department stores. If you opened one and rubbed the strip on your wrists, it was like putting on that expensive fragrance the stores wanted you to buy.

"But you stick the package in your purse," she said, "and use it on a special evening, just before you go into the room. Make yourself smell pretty."

Nettie continued, sympathetically, that she knew Liese couldn't afford perfume. Not that buying perfume was urgent in any case, she said, but Liese was young and so it probably mattered more to her than to her or Alvina. That's why they'd decided to give her the samples, instead of opening and trying them on as they usually did.

"Canada is a good country," Nettie said. "Before you know it, everything will be much better for you."

Liese had a small bottle of scent along but she didn't mention it. It was probably too cheap, and inappropriate, here. "Thank you Nettie," she said. "Thank you very much." In light of arriving in Canada and her relief at securing the name of this relative with the mole-marked face, the sacrifice of the samples seemed remarkable, much more than she deserved. Saying those thank yous, her voice began to break. Nettie patted her arm and said it was okay and she would leave her now, to unpack. She would soon call her for supper.

There wasn't much in Liese's two leather cases to hang up or put into drawers. When she was done, she undid one of the perfume packets and slipped the paper out of its sheath. It gave off a strong whiff of sophistication. She waited, contented, sitting on the bed, hands in her lap, eyes assessing the low-ceilinged room. She liked its simplicity, its coolness, its dimness. They didn't have many basements in the Chaco. A basement, she thought now, was like a cocoon in which she would be transformed for this world.

She heard Nettie's eager voice, the call for supper. She rubbed the paper against her wrists and ran upstairs, arriving at the table breathless and smiling. The cousins smiled back at her. Their hands were already folded for the table grace.

No one remarked on how she smelled, and when she casually brought an arm to her face, she couldn't smell the perfume either. It was clearly a tease, too little to last.

It didn't matter. The sensation of the strip against her skin, the brief fragrance of a Canadian ritual lingered with her as if it had rendered her newly exotic. And she was hungry and agreeable to everything. The cabbage soup and bread were delicious.

After supper, Liese helped with the dishes, then admitted she was tired. The cousins' voices wove around her like a lullaby, sung in duet, suggesting she get her pyjamas, take a bath, go to bed. Nettie and Alvina showed her the bathroom. Nettie asked if she knew how to turn on the taps and Liese said, yes, she did. Of course, she did, she added, though she kept her tone gracious and light. They had taps in the Chaco, she said. She didn't mention that they'd installed a water line into the kitchen just a few months ago, such a help to Mama, who had always drawn from a tap on the porch, but she did say that water was generally scarce in the Chaco so they showered instead of bathing, using a pail of water overhead—a pail with holes in it. Nettie and Alvina seemed to find this interesting.

Then the cousins withdrew, pulling the bathroom door closed behind them like a final caring cluck. Liese secured her hair in two loose braids. She took off her clothes. She drew an inch or two of tepid water and knelt in it, dabbing the water to her body until every part of it was moistened. Then she got out and dried herself and pulled on her thin summer nightgown. She padded downstairs and crawled between the starched and flawless white sheets of her basement bed.

Between those sheets, she lost the last pieces of her vivid daydream of the future. She knows this now, all these years later. It had begun to disappear the moment she landed, but the last of it disappeared in that very neat and proper bed. What did she surrender with her exhaustion, with that satisfied sigh just before sinking away—so carelessly—from everything, new and old colliding, into sleep?

She can't remember.

She should have written something down. She should have had a notebook on the flight, blocked that pesky girl from her lap, set down what she visualized ahead of her as her gaze and her dreams locked into the clouds. On the airplane, suspended in that space between ending and beginning, she must have known—in that clear way one sees what one wants before one

attains it—what she hoped for, what she expected. She was starting life over in a way more definite, more decisive, than people
usually did. Not escaping, but choosing. Switching countries.
Separating destiny from origin.

If she'd recorded this, she thinks now, she could decide
whether anything came true in the manner she had hoped. She
reminds herself that the landscape of her former desires can
never be fully recovered. It still adheres to a girl who hid, who
watched, who envied, and then to a young woman wrapped
in white. She no longer thinks of herself as an immigrant and
her reasons for coming are thin. As good as gone. And she may
never know, at this distance, if they were good enough.

Patricia Beach

Johnnie's grandparents sat in Puerto Casado for eight months before they decided that they had had enough. Every day for eight long months they told each other they would carry on. Every day they repeated their conviction that it was God who brought them to Paraguay, that the heat, the uncertainty, the problems with water, the fact that the land wasn't measured or the train line extended, that the Chaco grasslands contained only *Bittergras*, that their own infant daughter (the baby Maria) had been laid to rest in the port's Catholic cemetery, were simply tests of their faith. Tests they intended to persevere through, and pass.

His grandfather was not a *Prediger* or anyone high up, Johnnie says, but he was influential in his own way; people carried his statements from the evening conversations back to their makeshift beds for courage during nights of trying to sleep. His sentences were full of hope; they sounded green, so much better than the circumstances.

Eighty-three people had been carried to the grave by

September of 1927, and on the last day of that month, Johnnie's grandfather emerged for breakfast and announced that he and his family would return to Manitoba. They never laid eyes on the place they had come to settle. They never got past the port.

The story of his grandparents takes some time. Johnnie starts it when he and Liese turn onto Highway 59 out of Winnipeg. It uses up the whole hour north to Patricia Beach, where they are going for their first date. He pauses, sometimes, for miles, but Liese doesn't open a new conversation; she knows he's not finished.

"I wasn't there, of course," he says. "I'm trying to remember what they told us later."

Liese supposes Johnnie has chosen this topic because Paraguay is where she grew up. It's not even two years, in fact, since she came from there. It's an obvious connection, he's making it for her, and she's grateful. He seems pleased when she supplies a word, a name, a detail from her knowledge of the Mennonites at Puerto Casado, something with a German or Spanish tinge to it.

She has never been alone with Johnnie in a car, or, for that matter, with anyone she's this fond of. In Paraguay, young people courted on the churchyard after choir practice, or if things were heating up, in the fringes of the bush. Or they drove off, pressed close, on their small noisy motorcycles. She finds it strange and wonderful to sit on the cream-coloured seat beside him, skimming along the highway, just the two of them in his large sky-blue car. He says it's a Buick, but Betty, her friend who introduced them, calls it a boat. The wind is whistling through the inch of an opening he requires at the windows. Trees and fields and ditches high with grass flow past them in a steady line of green and brown.

Liese keeps turning to look at him, at his untidy mass of blond hair, the thick sideburns, his pale and handsome face roughened with a hint of beard. He's wearing sunglasses—aviator style.

This turning reminds her to listen, reminds her to anchor her mind from floating away in her happiness. Every time she turns, his head and shoulders move toward her for a moment, grow larger, blur, and then recede again. It's like watching missionary slides and waiting while the man at the projector presses a button to focus the picture of lepers or white-shirted preachers at some meetings or Bible school: the images surge in and out and then they're found as they should be, the edges sharp and the colours clear.

She tilts her head now and then, from habit, to loosen her hair. She runs her fingers through one side and then the other, checks—casually—that the rims of her ears haven't cracked her long straight hairdo apart. She was still in braids that day when she and Mama and Tina were eating watermelon under the *paraíso* tree and Tina cried, "Liese, your ears! They're on fire!" And Liese shrieked and clapped her hands against her head.

No, Tina explained when she had stopped laughing, Liese wasn't on fire, it was just the way she was sitting and her ears sticking out. They glowed so red when the sun came through them. Red, she said, and pink and orange. And Liese—such an innocent she was—asked if they actually stuck out and Mama *tsk*ed and said no, not that much, but Tina giggled and never stopped to consider what she'd done, turning her sister's ears into orbs—translucent, flammable orbs, appendages she felt she had to be mindful of from that time on, careful to set at certain angles and avoid setting at others, depending on her position and the sun. To keep her hair over them.

Johnnie's ears lie flat against his head. Liese has noticed this. They are perfectly even and oval, like apple slices, the half curl from stem to heart, the tidy round compartment in the middle, the hanging lobe.

"It wasn't easy," he's saying. "No one liked them for it at the port. People felt betrayed, of course."

"Of course."

"But then, the same thing here. They get back to Manitoba, subdued you know, all ready to agree with those who opposed the group that went. But they weren't welcomed back either! Snubbed, is more like it."

After a lengthy silence, Johnnie says, "It's really strange how these things work."

At Patricia Beach, Liese follows him along a narrow path, through trees, over a bit of a hill. And there it is. More water than she has ever seen.

Johnnie tells her Grand Beach is even better, but Patricia Beach is closest to the city and he wanted to take advantage of the time, coming after work and all. The nice thing is, there won't be many people.

It's true. They will have this part of the beach to themselves. An elderly couple is packing up. The man and the woman both smile at them in a friendly manner, as if to assure them that one is never too old for sand and sea. A young mother carrying straw bags in her hands and an inflated pink tube around her neck pushes past them toward the parking lot, her mouth set in a grim straight line. Two small children toddle after her, whimpering.

Johnnie spreads a blue-and-red-checked blanket on the sand. He takes off his tattered tennis shoes and sets them neatly behind the blanket. He stretches out on his stomach and sighs with contentment.

Liese sits down beside him, knees pulled up, hands crossed around her legs. Johnnie nods at the cooler. "Help yourself," he says.

There's Coca Cola, potato chips, and store-bought cookies. Liese has never been to the beach, so Johnnie brought everything.

Propped on his elbows, Johnnie doodles in the sand. He makes a square, a circle, a triangle. He links them with loops and wavy lines. Liese watches him. His hands are wide and the fingers seem muscular, if such a thing is possible. Now that they've arrived at the beach, she's waiting for a new conversation.

But Johnnie isn't through with his grandparents yet. "Just think," he says, "if my grandparents had stayed with the group that went down in '27, I would have met you earlier. In Paraguay."

He looks at her and grins. "We might be having a picnic on the other side of the world! Is there a lake, a beach, nearby?"

"No lake," she says slowly. "Just a tiny park... On the ranches there are dugouts. Some people swim in the dugouts... But nothing like this. Not like this at all."

"I think it's neat." He emphasizes *neat*, as if he chose it especially for her. "I mean, I find it fascinating, to think how my life might have turned out if my grandfather hadn't come out of that tent and said, We're going back."

He traces, deepens, his sand figures, in the same order he drew them. "Have you ever wondered," he says, "what your life would be like if someone in your past had made a different decision?"

Liese thinks she's falling in love with Johnnie, so she wants to be careful. "Well," she says, "I guess I've wondered ... sometimes, what if my mother had won. For a while there, when there was such an exodus from the colony, she told me she'd been quite desperate to pick up and move to Canada too. But my father wouldn't hear of it... Yeah, so I've thought about it. A little. Getting here sooner."

"Do you think we'd be the same people?" he asks. "The same if we were, say, sitting on a blanket in your tiny park in the Chaco of Paraguay? Would our history have changed us, you know what I mean? Or is personality—the essential existence of us—the same?"

He carries on, without waiting for her reply. "For what it's worth," he says, "I think I'd be the same, you know, no matter where! I used to daydream in school. I'd imagine myself in all sorts of situations—in places I'd read about, and other times. Even thousands of years ago. And I was one and the same. That's how it felt to me."

"We'd be quite different," she says.

She'd intended this to sound musing and tentative, but the entire sentence has emerged in one breath; her statement is absolute. Her failure frightens her, so she bolts on. "We wouldn't have met in Paraguay," she says. "Never. You would have been from Menno Colony and I'm from Fernheim. We wouldn't have met, or had a picnic. Not there."

Johnnie rolls onto his back, joins his hands under his head, fixes his eyes on her. "Really?" he says. "Why not?" He's smiling. It seems he really wants to know.

She turns from his gaze and hopes he'll think she's considering it. The truth is, she's annoyed. She picks a twig off the sand, breaks it in two, then each half in two again.

So he's fascinated. So he thinks it's neat. History as a whim. Their near-connection. Their near-miss. He thinks it's neat and she feels like saying, if you really want to know, your past and mine, your grandparents, well the expression in German is, *Es macht mir zu schaffen*. It's too much work, she wants to say, an idea like yours.

She knows her Mennonite history; Johnnie doesn't have to show off about that. Russia-Canada-Paraguay: his triangle on the sand. His family and hers, moving along the lines of it. They're all Mennonites, yes, but his fled Russia half a century before hers were ready to leave. Then they ran scared of the world again, just when they were nicely established in Manitoba and Saskatchewan. There was the Chaco. Huge and empty. Nobody there but nomadic Indians.

Her people, barely getting out when Russia betrayed them. Too late for Canada. Her mother complaining that only Paraguay was left, what choice did they have? In her father's version, God knew in advance and wanted them exactly where they were. He had to admit that God's will, in this case, required the conservatives from Canada finding the Chaco first. But that shouldn't be construed as a recommendation of their fellow colonists, who seemed to him different and intransigent. Even the Pharoah discharged the purposes of God, he said.

So Johnnie believes they would have found one another? Anywhere? "Well, why not in Russia?" she says. "Maybe in some coal mine or forest of the north. A picnic under the trees. If the guard doesn't catch and kill us first."

Johnnie's smile retreats slightly; visibly. Liese feels unrepentant. She can't believe he's so ignorant of, so unaware of the splits along the way. He can be thankful she hasn't dragged out the words education, culture, progressive, to hurt him. His speculations are useless. Only one point—*this* one point—is available to them.

"We wouldn't have met anywhere else," she says. "We've met because your grandparents came back and I moved here too."

Because, she's thinking, we're outsiders of sorts, your grandparents and I. We're quitters.

But she has no wish to be rolled into a lump of dough with some old people of his genealogy. Not yet. "Can't we talk about something else?" she asks. "I was hoping we could, maybe, talk about us... Our lives here."

She is answered with silence, an unthreatening silence no heavier than a feather would be, brushing over sand. Still, it's silence and it weakens her, makes her apprehensive. Now she notices the hair on Johnnie's arm, how white it is, and the smell of him, perspiration mixed with whatever he puts on after shaving. She wishes she could lean into his chest, the way she used to press her face into the screen of the kitchen door when it was raining. She watched storms through all their stages, rewarded at the end with the sharp fresh aroma of washed brick and damp soil.

"Okay," he says at last. "Let's talk about here." His tone is even, he sounds fine with it, as if he hasn't noticed her exasperation, as if his long pause was an accident. "Winnipeg, Manitoba. Canada. Why not?"

He leads off: his job at the furniture plant. Then hers at the seniors' home. The weather, her cousins Nettie and Alvina, their mutual friends. Liese feels their conversation become animated and amusing. She finds the words she wants when she wants them; her English, she feels, is going well.

Johnnie brought a ball so after a while they get up and pass it back and forth. It's a soft yellow ball. They throw it gently, making it impossible for the other to miss. The ball makes a light slapping noise on their hands. Liese laughs when she sends it off to him and when she receives it.

Gradually they wander toward the water. They move in, step by step, throw by throw, until the water is halfway up their legs. The lake is surprisingly warm.

Liese warned Johnnie before they left that she doesn't swim, and he said that was fine, going to the beach wasn't necessarily about swimming. She even told him she doesn't have a swimsuit, though she's been looking for one. That was fine as well.

But now he wants to swim. "You don't mind, do you?"

"No. No, really. Let me see how you swim."

He strips off his shirt and tosses it onto the sand. He wades into the water. When he is waist-deep, he leaps forward and swims away. He doesn't look back, or say goodbye. Liese watches him until he's a speck on the lake surface, until she loses sight of him.

Seated on the blanket, Liese tries to find Johnnie again. Sometimes she's sure she's spotted him, but then she thinks she sees him elsewhere and there's no thread between the two places. The sun lowers gradually on her left, water and sky exchanging colours and appearance. The sky darkens, becomes a solid backdrop, and the water grows lighter, more luminous. It springs, shimmering, away from her gaze.

It seems to her that Johnnie is swimming a very long time. Could something be wrong? But he leapt in with too much power and confidence to be in trouble.

Perhaps he's swimming away from her.

She debates this. She reviews his expression and his bearing as he turned. Her last comment, she decides, was dumb. Let me see how you swim. As if Lake Winnipeg were a pond he would circle for her benefit. He doesn't like her after all, that's it; he regretted the date, he paddled in a vast arc to some other point down the beach and then walked to his car. He could be roaring down the highway in his Buick-boat at this moment, glad to be away from her.

Liese shivers. She eats a cookie. She takes Johnnie's towel, wraps it around her shoulders and arms like a shawl. She raises her knees, puts her head down onto her towel-clad arms, into the warmth and soap scent of the nubby cloth.

It was her outburst about their histories, the chance of them meeting. That's what his absence represents. Her sarcasm. She let her irritation show.

But the argument immediately revives itself within her. Don't tell me, she thinks, there's not an ocean's voyage and then some between *Brüdergemeinde* and *Sommerfelder*. Between *Russländer* and *Kanadier*. Between the Fernheim and Menno colonies. The two of us, she thinks, are from other sides and Mennonite social subtleties all the long way back to Russia. Who knows, going even further back, one of us is probably Frisian and the other Flemish.

Can she help that she's imagined marrying him? Can she help that the complications were immediately clear, that they confused her? Her parents will have things to say. His too, most likely. People say things! These differences matter.

She isn't ready for the past, that's all. Not his, not hers. She wanted to drive away with Johnnie from the places they had been. Over an hour to Patricia Beach and all she got was Abram and Elisabeth Braun. Or was it Peter, Maria, Heinrich, Anna, Martin, Jakob, Katharina? Had he even mentioned their names?

She hadn't explained, and so it came out wrong, and now he's refusing to come back to her. She pushes her head harder against her knees, angry. How many times did her mother warn and scold her. "You have to learn everything the hard way, don't you, Lieschen, and then you miss what you really want."

She tries to relax, tries pleading. I can live with it, she promises. I'll find out their reasons, tell him mine. Once we have the details out in the air, I'll be able to connect us as simply as he does, locate us together. Anywhere.

Anything, she moans in a whisper, if I can only have him back. Anything.

She's being melodramatic and she knows it, but her desperation feels genuine. It's why I came, she moans. Go to Canada and find yourself a husband, girl. Remember?

She's startled by a sound, like a nesting bird frightened into flight directly in front of her. She lifts her head.

Johnnie is walking out of the water, dripping and tugging at his trunks as if to realign himself. "That was great!" he exclaims.

Liese quickly unwraps the towel.

"Were you cold?" he asks.

"A little."

"Keep it then. I'll put my shirt over."

"No." She jumps up. "No. You need to dry off. Here."

The brown towel remains between them. He shrugs it away. "I'll dry in the air."

"Take it, Johnnie," she begs.

Again her intensity has surprised him. "Hey," he cautions, "it's not that serious."

"Sorry." Her hand with the towel drops. "Honestly, I am."

Johnnie stares at her, then laughs. "At the risk of offending you, Liese," he says, "I don't think we could have missed each other, even in opposite colonies in Paraguay."

She wonders, for a fleeting moment, what it will be like for them, neither one able to give in, but she can't consider that now: her worries have been silly and needless. Johnnie didn't swim away from her; he's back.

"Take the towel!" she orders. But she's joking now and he knows it. He reaches for the towel. She grabs it away. He lunges at her, but she's too quick for him. He wants it now, and she won't let him have it. She holds it out, he tries again. She runs.

She feels the strength and elegance of her legs, teasing swiftly away from him over the moist brown beach. She's well ahead of him, the towel tucked under her arm like a taunt.

He chases, feet thudding behind her, and he's gaining. He catches her. Of course.

"Now I'm dry," he says. He swings her around. "And I don't need it!"

"And I'm warm," she pants. "I don't need it either." She wedges the towel under his arm.

With one smooth movement Johnnie removes it and flips it behind him and over his shoulder and pulls her into the shelter it makes. "Then we'll both use it," he says.

Liese takes her end of the towel and he holds his. Their free arms circle the other's waist. They walk back slowly, and slowly they regain their breath. The sun is dropping away behind a wide bank of orange and silver clouds in the west. The water is a field of shining pebbles, the band of sand is a path. When she writes her parents, she'll tell them about Patricia Beach. She'll describe it as accurately as she can. How beautiful it is.

For herself, she's going to remember Johnnie's damp trunks marking one side of her, and his strong broad hand the other.

Mama, Like a Mirage

That winter, the year Robert turns one, Anita Johnson—the woman from the church who's befriended Liese—starts doing exercises every morning with a television show and walking three or four times a week regardless of the weather, and then she joins a woman's health club called a spa. She's "into" fitness, she says, and Liese, who still struggles with English prepositions on occasion, finds it odd that Anita would talk about her relentless activity as if it's a tunnel she crawls inside.

Maybe that's how it is when you get so busy with something and it's all you can see, she thinks. Until you're into something else. She wonders aloud if she'll be abandoned too.

Johnnie says she's being unreasonable. "You're friends," he says.

"She can't resist. I'm new. I need her expertise."

"Oh jeez," he says. "Why are you always suspicious?"

Johnnie, she thinks, is glad for whoever shows up, never mind quality. Or durability.

Then Anita calls and says she has a guest pass and would Liese want to join her for the evening? "I know you'll love it, Louise," she says, using the English version of Liese's name. "You're not overweight or anything, I know, but it's more than that. It's about overall fitness. Feeling energetic and really refreshed. You wouldn't believe how much better I feel since I've been going. Not just physically better, but in every single way."

She pauses but Liese doesn't say anything so she hurries on. "Plus you'll have some idea of what I'm up to, you know what I mean? You'll be able to visualize the place."

"Well…" Liese can't tell her the reasons she doesn't want to go. Not, at least, the ones that come to her first. She can't say, I'd rather not because it's dark outside. Or, you've called me as a last resort, haven't you?

"I know it's short notice," Anita is saying, as if she can hear what Liese is thinking. "I meant to call you earlier, but today's been such a whirl!"

She can't say winter is hard for her, that it's summer in Paraguay now, where she grew up, and no one ever believes you could miss the heat. She can't say that she's still unnerved by unfamiliar situations.

Anita will think she needs to console her. She'll repeat her name to show how much she cares. "But Louise," she'll say, "you've been here five years already. And think of it, Louise, how awfully much courage it took for you to come. How brave and strong you've been."

Their friendship has too many sentences like that in it.

"I'll check with Johnnie," she says.

The table is cluttered with dishes, the brown stoneware plates, his and hers, their orange sunflowers streaked with gravy, looking even more grotesque than before they'd spooned their suppers onto them. She'd exclaimed over the set when they got it as a wedding gift but she despises it now. Eating on those fat showy petals day after day.

A chunk of meatball has fallen onto the seat of Robert's high-chair. There's a pickle on the floor, just out of her reach. And the curtains aren't drawn for the night. This never bothers Johnnie. "We're on the second floor," he says, "so who's looking in?" One of the hooks is off the rod and a narrow ridge of ice lines the bottom of the window.

Liese sees the letter-in-progress to her parents, the pale blue aerogram, so light, so insubstantial, lying on the spindly-legged coffee table they picked up cheap at a garage sale. But oh how heavy with endeavour it is: such careful words, so cramped and slanted, composed about anything she can think of that may be informative or lend itself to further elaboration, every line tucked closely under the last. To make it worth sending.

Once a month, a letter home. When you leave home, Liese knows, you have to reassure your mother.

"Up to you," Johnnie says when she whispers the invitation. "I can do the dishes, put Robert to bed."

Her hand is clamped over the phone. Why can't she make a simple decision, make a simple statement that yes, she'll come, or no, she won't, but thanks for asking?

The aerogram shimmers in her vision, seems urgent. She's run out of things to say, but if she goes along with Anita, she may have enough new material to finish the letter. There's bound to be something at a spa that will interest her parents.

Then she sees Robert reach for Johnnie's pant leg, sees Johnnie tug the boy onto his lap and fold his arms around him without taking his eyes off the television, sees her little one's blond head nuzzling his father's neck, Johnnie's nose in the child's hair. The sight pierces her with pleasure and resolution, as if leaving for the evening could fix them in that affectionate arrangement forever. Liese takes her hand off the mouthpiece. "Yes," she says. "I'll come."

But she hasn't expected—behind the industrial steel doors of that building, windowless—the spa to be pink. It's pink and summery and cheerful, and there's music playing, and it all seems new, barely unwrapped. The carpet is pink. The wallpaper, lockers, and draperies are pink. The stool at the water fountain and the counter to their right. Large mirrors toss the rosy colour around the room like foam.

"Everything's pink," she says.

Anita laughs. "I know! Isn't it pretty?"

Exercise machines in gleaming chrome line three walls of the spacious room. There's a nook at the far side of it with two white wicker tables and matching chairs with pink cushions and on the wall a banner cries, "Let's be shapely!" The exclamation mark is a string of hearts.

"Well, they've sure spent money," she blurts. Stupidly, of course, because just a week ago Anita mentioned that Liese talks about money a lot. She'd noted this with a tone of sadness, so Liese felt compelled to receive her observation as a kindness. She should try a little harder to trust God for all of her needs, Anita said, and Liese agreed that she should.

A young woman in a black leotard is working one of the machines. It's a rope attached to a pulley that she lifts high over her head, then drags to the ground. Black rectangular weights clank against the top of the contraption behind her as she touches the floor and then they plummet down as her arm and body move back up. She and the weights are opposite and inseparable. Up and down they flow, reaching like praise and scraping like contrition, again and again without a break in the rhythm.

Liese is holding her breath, wishing the woman would stop. But she doesn't stop and with each smooth and downward bend her hair flings behind her, as if breathless too, as if in awe. Her hair is bleached and very white and when it lands against the pink of the rug it seems a tiny explosion, like a party sparkler going off.

Liese senses Anita watching her and so she turns and shrugs. "It's so unexpected," she says. "In winter."

Anita signs her name in her flowery script in a large date book on the counter. The receptionist is absorbed in a magazine. Anita clears her throat.

"I've brought a guest," she says proudly, as if Liese is a gift. The receptionist jumps up and it's "Hello, hello, hello!" like tiny bells. "My name's Cherie."

Cherie is bony-thin but her dark hair is long and glossy and it surges about her shoulders as she moves. She says it's fantastic that Liese has come and hopes she'll have an amazingly wonderful time. She sounds excited. She says the only purpose of the spa is to make everyone feel better.

"Anita here," she says, glancing at the name in the sign-in book, "is one of our members and I'm sure she's already told you how much fun she has."

Liese nods.

"So let's get you measured for your personalized workout chart. See what you'll want to work on. Then I'll let Anita take you around, through the starters' routine."

"She doesn't have an extra pound," Anita tells Cherie.

"Doesn't look that way." Cherie rounds the counter to take a closer look and Liese holds herself as narrow as possible.

"But it's not just weight loss," the receptionist says. "It's tone and energy and feeling good. Up to our best."

She tips her head closer and lowers her voice. "And none of us minds improving our bust line, do we?"

Liese blushes.

She doesn't like to be measured, but it seems another thing she has to learn to accept. "We women don't accept ourselves the way we should," Anita has told her more than once. "That's the answer to the women's lib stuff everyone's talking about. Really saying Yes to our bodies, our sex, our femininity. To all that we are. To stop minding who we are! To say yes!"

Liese thinks yes as Cherie pulls the white tape around her bust, her waist, her hips, her thighs, as she says the numbers aloud to Anita who repeats them like prices while she records them on a small pink card. She worries about the other women seeing the tight patch of skin above her left elbow where she burned herself at the wood stove when she was five, the scar on her leg from the motorcycle accident, the freckles on her arms.

"My stomach isn't flat," she mutters. "Still from my baby."

"We'll work that tummy away in no time at all," Cherie says. She pats Liese's abdomen but it feels like a gust of dust in her face and Liese jerks away.

Anita and Liese begin their workout at the stationary bicycles. They mount pink seats and begin to ride. They laugh.

Liese is over her surprise, she's adjusting. She asks Anita what she should do with her eyes. A mirror covers the wall in front of them and it seems rude to look at her friend or the other bodies in the room with their reflected buttocks and breasts and what-not-all bouncing. But to look at herself? Her long white legs and coppery hair? The mirror would break if you stared too long, her sister Tina used to say.

"Do you look at yourself?" she asks.

"Louise!" Anita exclaims, glancing at her in the mirror. Joyfully, it seems. "The questions you have! You're priceless!"

This is the way she wants it, Liese thinks, *this* way, for a friendship. Alert to the other's absurdity. The other's uniqueness.

"Hey," Anita goes on, "do what you want. Smile at yourself. Look around. Close your eyes."

Liese closes her eyes. Music pours out of loudspeakers in the ceiling, pours out like a gush of water, classical, rousing, and glorious. Music for a noble cause. She's positive, diligent, flexible. Once again she's here; she's arrived.

They work their way from the bicycles to the various machines around the room, one after the next to tone one body part after the other. Liese lowers herself onto a bench, on her back, the way Anita showed her, grasping the handholds of the rod over her head. She'll push the rod and its attached weights—the designated number for a beginner—up to the full stretch of her arms.

She turns her head and sees Mama. The back of her. The rounded shape, the shoulders, the soft yellow-grey hair twisted neatly in a bun at her neck. She's riding a bicycle. There's no mistaking her mother.

Liese springs up from the bench as if released from a trap, "Ma!" about to leap from her throat. Their eyes meet.

Liese sees the round and ponderous face. It's not her mother's. The cheeks are rouge-reddish at the peaks and the woman's mouth is different too. Wider.

But I saw her and she saw me. Our eyes touched and I'm filled with ecstasy and then I'm filled with anger, that she's up to her tricks. Following me. Not wanting me to leave, then saying I have to, and when I come and when I stay, she's not pleased with it either. A visit, she said, just a visit! Well, I've married and what can you do, changing countries, falling in love? Yes, I know she loves Johnnie too, as much as she can from afar, from pictures. Her hunger for baby Robert like a dirge through every line of her letters.

My heart pounding and angry, nearly hugging a large woman with rouge on a bicycle, and planning to shout, "What are you doing here?" Swinging her arms while she rides, not holding the handlebars, just like she propelled herself over the yard from kitchen to milk shed, as if she meant to scatter the flies and the heat in a long wide swath.

"I don't run after stuff like this," I would have said, whether
Anita heard me or not. "All this puffing and panting. I'm here as a
guest. It's my first time. I know how silly and shallow it must look
to you, Mama, but there's more to Canada than this!"

It isn't Mama. This happens, the eyes fooled, the brain fooled
for a second by a passing resemblance. Mama, like a mirage. But
the brief, false sighting reels me in like a real visitation, and I don't
know what she wants. Who appears in places like this? Angels or
enemies? Would Mama ever indulge herself this way? I only really
saw her body once. In her underwear. I averted my eyes, fastened
my gaze on her legs, below the knees, brown as weathered leather,
but then I was moved by curiosity. It seemed as if she were another
species then, and I let myself look further, as far as the untanned
thighs. Her legs there a bluish white like skim milk, veins criss-
crossing them. A ghastly sight, it seemed to me, and enormous: the
contrasting colours, the bulging flesh.

She said she used to be slender. She had a photograph of herself
as a younger woman. "Younger and smaller," she would say with
satisfaction, lifting the photo out of her box of keepsakes, and I'd
hold the photograph with both hands, afraid to lose or damage it,
as if it was the only proof she had of herself. But I didn't study it
as she must have hoped I would, just glanced at it and held it and
handed it back.

"Be glad you have your father's frame," she told me. "No wider
than kindling. When it's hot the sweat runs and my legs rub and
it hurts to walk."

I stepped barefoot on a cactus spike and Mama soaked my foot
in very hot water and then she set me into the bright light of the
verandah and removed the thorn with a needle and her fingers.
She showed it to me, the evidence of what she had done, but my
heel throbbed as if the thorn was still there, even deeper than
before. She took my hand and went inside and I hobbled after her.
She sat down on a chair and I climbed onto her wide rolling lap. I

let her hold me in her arms while I cried. I let her rock me. I must have been eight or nine then, a big girl.

"This feels wonderful for mothers too, you know," she said, whispering as if I was her infant child. So I pushed myself up and away from her. I set my injured foot on the tile floor and it felt cool to the touch. It felt like needles, but I let it take my weight. "Child!" she cried, for she must have seen my grimace, and I lied and said, "It doesn't hurt anymore."

Next time, Mama, come back to me singing, as I remember you from very young, when I tried to isolate your voice from the other women's voices around me in church, when I tried to shut out everything but your soprano, as if it were an uncommonly melodious birdsong. Until I was a few years older and sat on a pew with my friends and heard it, too loud, too penetrating now. Pious like a prayer. Checking us over on the way to church with a frown and those judging clicks between your teeth, pinching and poking, straightening collars and rubbing dusty spots with a moistened finger. Then singing the hymns with abandon as if you'd never been dissatisfied with any of us. I felt the gap and my own judgments took root.

Come back, I wanted to say, and listen. I'll explain everything. I'll explain why I'm here in this very pink place.

They've showered and dressed and Anita says, "We'll have to stop and talk to Cherie for a few minutes before we go, remember? She'd like to chat about spa plans and specials. Your program and stuff. They do that with visitors."

Liese doesn't answer.

"Listen, Louise, don't think I'm trying to push you into joining. I'd really like you to sign up too and I think it's the greatest and everything, but I'm not trying to pressure you. Really. I know you're saving to get out of the apartment. Maybe you want to think of yourself too, but there's no pressure. Sure, we get benefits if our guests sign up, but it's not much, maybe a tote bag or something. Maybe something off our fees. But that's not why I'm bringing my friends. Okay?"

"I know."

So they sit at the white table in the pink alcove while Cherie unfolds brochures outlining the history of the spa movement, the string of shops across the continent, the ten-year, five-year, one-year plans. The three-month trial. The various ways to pay: cash or monthly installments. How little it costs per day.

Liese nods as Cherie talks, willing her to hurry.

There's an album of photographs—women "before and after." They're more attractive in their second picture; slimmer. They no longer seem discouraged.

Liese says, "I'll never be fat. My mother is fat, but I'm more like my father's side and—"

For the first time Cherie's eyes are hard instead of professionally patient. "We don't use the word *fat* around here." Then, more slowly, she says, "We're not just about weight loss." The weary forbearance in her voice suggests that the complexities of their program—even the rudiments, in fact— are beyond Liese's grasp. "It's about tone and energy and feeling better." She reaches into a cupboard behind her for another binder, opens it to studies, numbers, and graphs. To connections of health and membership. Her voice is a mono-tone now. She has to get through it.

Liese can't concentrate. Anita's here, why isn't she helping her as she usually does? She wants to leave her friend to this pitch and search the room for the woman she mistook for her mother. See what she's doing now. Playing jump-rope, maybe. That would be a treat, Mama jumping rope!

She wants to know what they exchanged in that look, unfold and wrap it again with everything good, settling the miles between them, heart to heart. She wants to find the words for the last paragraphs of the letter, not anything about the spa but memories now: dear Mama, dear Mama, dear Mama.

There's a question in the air. It's Cherie. She's asking Liese if she understands.

She's floating away from a dream and says "Yes" with a passion that startles her but seems to please Cherie, who says, "So which plan will you take?"

"Which plan?" Like an echo.

"I'd like you to choose the plan that works for you."

Liese has no intention of returning. Not as a member. Not as a guest.

"I don't know, I ... "

Cherie steals a glance at her watch. It's late, near closing time. She's tired too. "Which plan appeals to you most?"

"I ... I ... would have to talk to my husband."

"Of course you'll want to consult him, but I'd like you to select one plan tonight, whether you sign up this evening or not. Then when you come again, we'll have something to work with."

"I'm not coming back." She's not looking at Cherie but at the pink trim on her sleeve.

Anita finally opens her mouth. Her voice is brisk and confiding. "Louise has never seen a spa, Cherie. She's from Paraguay. Paraguay, South America. She's an immigrant."

Immigrant. The label Liese needs to shed more than pounds. As if she's Anita's very own trinket, needing a polish.

But Liese is run-down from everything—the exercise, the sales pitch, Mama surprising her—and she lowers her head and lets it bend over her.

"I know she doesn't look Spanish," Anita is saying. "She's not. It's really interesting, actually. There are colonies of Germans in Paraguay. So she looks Canadian—white, you know—but she's actually Paraguayan. It's really quite different in Paraguay and you have to imagine how new and strange things are for her. Over here. She really *will* have to think about it."

Anita stands. "We had a wonderful time, both of us did." She's efficient, she's gracious. "Thank you for letting me bring her as my guest. And thank you for going over the program with us. It's been such a lovely evening. I'm thrilled to be a member."

It's too much confident charm, even for Anita, but Liese lets the words go, lets them spin around her confused and caught-out self.

Anita turns. "We had a wonderful time, didn't we, Louise?"

Their escape is imminent, and it wasn't Mama after all. Liese thinks she can match Anita, give her and Cherie something for their efforts.

"I liked it," she says. "I liked it so very much. I had a wonderful, wonderful time."

Evangeline

She's nearly finished the third-floor hallway, but she had to dash away for a minute to check on the children, napping in their apartment on the floor below. When she returns, the vacuum cleaner is gone and its long black cord is slithering into a doorway halfway down the hall.

"Hey!" Liese yells. She bolts there but the door is shut.

The plug and a foot or so of the cord got stuck and are still outside the door. She knocks. The tenants in this suite are new. She hasn't met them, doesn't know their names. A couple, she thinks. If the cord is damaged, if she doesn't get the vacuum cleaner back, she and Johnnie will have to replace it. They can't afford it.

They can't afford anything.

Liese knocks again. She thinks she's being watched through the peephole.

"That's the landlord's vacuum cleaner," she says loudly to the tiny eye.

Silence.

Liese steps aside, out of the peephole's range. She stomps her feet as if she's walking away, then lowers herself to the floor close to the wall and slides her hands to the plug, grabs on to it. She waits.

She kneels there, waiting, more than ten minutes by her watch, and her knees begin to ache and her hands grow numb and she feels the panic rising inside her because of her children alone in the apartment, locked in, yes, but possibly waking, calling for her. And fear that someone will emerge into this hallway and see her, perched on the floor, and what will she say if they do? And because of everything else, the throbbing frustration of the place, the intensity of so much going on around her, the way they're cramped into their four rooms, anonymous in a way but never free of people either. There are other immigrants from Paraguay in the building, just like her, and she can hardly bear it anymore, the way they sit in their lawn chairs summer evenings, on the patch of grass at the street or on the steps, sipping their cold Paraguayan tea, or their beer, their Low German rabble raucous in the air, the familiarity of it all and the reek of perspiration.

She's waiting, tense inside and out.

Then a pop and a sucking sound, and the door opens, barely an inch. Liese feels a tug and the slack she's allowed the cord tightens. The door opens wider and she frog-jumps forward, yanking on the cord and forcing the door with her shoulder. The door hits the cylinder of the cleaner and stops. There's a woman standing beside it, about her age, Liese guesses. She's small and her hair is long and dark, askew on her shoulders. She's wearing a turquoise quilted housecoat, its belt tight around her waist and tied in a knot.

Liese has the impression of fine taut features, just a glimpse of blue in the eyes, of dark lashes and brows, flashes of colour against the stark lightness of her skin, but flashing away from her like a fish in a tank, for the woman has folded over immediately, not looking at her but pushing the awkward appliance toward her and scrabbling at the hose, trying to free the cord that's still caught under the door. The woman's hands are shaking. "Take it, take it," she says, her voice surprisingly strong, but ragged as her hair.

Liese is thinking about the children. Robert may be calling for her, or crying, wanting out of his crib. This is such a waste of her time.

"What are you're doing?" she barks. "Taking my vacuum cleaner? It's the landlord's, you know, and I've got to do the hallway!"

"To use," the other woman says, still bent, "to use. Take it, take it."

She speaks in twos and her sentences are bare-boned as if she may be an immigrant as Liese has been.

She'll equal her then. "You stealing! You stealing!" she says.

"Who's there, darling?" A dark, slow voice, as if out of sleep. A man's voice, sounding older and weary.

Liese notices the heat of the apartment now and some cloying smell like onions and perfume.

The woman has dropped to her knees, still pushing at the machine and the yards of cord curled about in the tiny entrance, and her efforts are forcing Liese back. But she doesn't trust the woman and can't let go of the plug.

"Evangeline, darling, what's all the noise about? Can't you be still? Can't you be quiet?" His voice distant, it seems, though no farther away than the living room, and seductive, sentences like fingers reaching around the small frightened woman on the floor. Still wearing her housecoat in the afternoon! It's as if she can't hear him, or pays no attention, fluttering as if she's in a cage and restless for escape, and then Liese has it, the cord is free and the whole contraption is out. She's flushed backward along with the beast and the door is once again shut in her face.

It's going on five years, she and Johnnie in the apartment on Edison Avenue, in the two-bedroom on the second floor of one of the three-storey walkups built in a flurry of construction over the decade to replace old houses on over-sized lots. Thoughtless rezoning, she mutters to herself every time she goes for a walk, turning the neighbourhood—once half rural and given to market gardening and small-scale chicken farming—into a mishmash of human habitation: houses from various eras, new side-by-sides, and apartment buildings, like an irregular heartbeat, every street a series of changing moods.

Their building is powder blue and U-shaped, early seventies, so fairly new. Ken-Bet Apartments. Someone said it was named after the couple that owns the building and this offends Liese, that this unknown Ken and Betty or Betsy own the hive she and Johnnie have to live in; get rich off them, no doubt. Liese refers to the building by number, not by its name.

Not that it hasn't suited them well enough, not that it isn't part of their plan. But it's taking so much longer than they expected to get into a house of their own and she's despairing of it.

Last summer, their fourth year in the apartment, the caretaker moved out and Liese got the job of cleaning the hallways and foyer every day but Sunday, for a reduction in rent. Afternoons, she puts Robert and Amelia down for their nap, locks the door, vacuums the hallway on one wing of the building, hurries back to their apartment, unlocks the door, and listens. If the children are still asleep, she runs back and does the hallway on the other side. And so it goes, back and forth, all three floors. She usually manages to get it done while the children sleep, but the procedure makes her tense.

Johnnie sometimes asks why she doesn't do it when the children are awake. Liese reminds him that the building manager wants the vacuuming done in the afternoon. Some people like to sleep mornings, he said, and evenings they're coming and going and he doesn't want them inconvenienced. Other tenants are waiting for the cleaning job if she can't handle it, he said.

Johnnie says, "After their naps, I mean. It's still afternoon. Take them with you."

She's explained the reasons more than once. "Having them run up and down, sure, shrieking and banging on doors, getting in the way! As if that will work!"

And it's too much noise for their so-young ears. "Have you ever listened to that thing?" she says. "It's like a plane taking off."

"I thought these better ones were supposed to be quiet."

"Compared to what?

And so it goes when she's complaining, with variations. He doesn't understand either why she keeps running back to check on the children. Don't they sleep long enough for her to get it done?

Usually they do, she says, but sometimes they don't. She'd never forgive herself if something happened to them. Who knows what triggers their waking? "They're in the same room, you know, so if Amelia cries, Robert does too. He's trying to climb out of his crib all the time."

The boy is ready for a regular bed, she reminds Johnnie; he needs a room of his own. As if Johnnie doesn't know.

The vacuum belongs to the landlord, but they keep it in their apartment. It fills up the bottom of their front closet. They're allowed to use it for their personal cleaning. It's one of those so-called superior models sold by salesmen coming into homes. Before she had the caretaking job and access to the landlord's vacuum, she had signed up for an in-home demonstration. Johnnie sat through the sales pitch with her but he was annoyed. He clutched the free knives they got for letting the salesman come and glared at the soft layer of downy dust the machine sucked up from their mattress with disbelief, as if there was a trick in it he'd missed while blinking. Then he said their little vacuum cleaner would do the same if they'd ever thought of vacuuming the mattress. Liese was ashamed of his rudeness.

When the salesman set the hose to a patch of the living-room carpet that she'd vacuumed just that day, she thought she could see the difference his machine made, but Johnnie couldn't see it at all. Then he declared they really weren't interested, and couldn't afford it either, and when Liese turned to him in disappointment, he said, in front of the man, who was young and nervous and clearly learning his routine, "Listen, Liese, will it be a down-payment or will it be a vacuum cleaner?"

The vacuums were expensive, and so he had her cornered.

They've been arguing a lot this year and she blames the apartment. The way it forces them together.

Or maybe it's because they're close to reaching their house down-payment goal. They're within a year now, they think, of having enough. A year that's lasting forever. As if it's a marathon and they can't get there without this constant pain. These repetitive exchanges. Like spatters of mud, like a truck driving through a puddle near their otherwise decent relationship.

Liese is pleased she rescued the vacuum cleaner, finished the hallways, and then the children awake, as delighted to see her as she is to see them, and while she's giving them a snack, the telephone rings and it's the mechanic at the garage where Johnnie left the car this morning. They've found the problem, he says. It will be about $600 to fix it. She swallows and says what she knows Johnnie would say: they need the car, so do what it takes. She feels her stomach churning, feels their goal sliding back by two months.

Johnnie brings home two raspberry jelly doughnuts left over from a meeting at work. He grabs one of them, kisses her and says the other doughnut is for her. She says she'll save it for later and tells him what the mechanic said. He shrugs. "It's what I expected," he says.

"You said it was something small."

He shrugs again. "Fixing a car, $600 is small."

After supper, Johnnie plays with Robert and Amelia while Liese does the dishes. Then she walks to the grocery store two blocks away. Going, shopping, returning, while the sky in the west shifts prettily with the pastels of sunset, Liese looks forward to eating the doughnut. Maybe he'll have the kids tucked in, she thinks, and they'll watch a comedy or something and she'll eat her doughnut and they'll have sex and (either before or after) they'll comfort one another about the bill from the garage. They'll get a good night's sleep. They'll face tomorrow, tomorrow.

But the children are still in their day clothes and fussing and Johnnie's absorbed in something on the television and then she notices, the doughnut is gone.

Liese drops the bag of groceries on the counter harder than she needs to. "Where's my doughnut?" she says.

"What doughnut?"

"My doughnut. You brought me a doughnut and I was saving it."

"I figured you didn't want it," he said. "So I ate it."

"Jeepers."

"It's not as if you need it, Liese."

She doesn't want the children to hear them quarrel so she sidles beside him on the sofa and says, under her breath, "And what is *that* supposed to mean?"

"I mean I didn't attach importance to that doughnut as *your* doughnut and since we'd had other dessert—that pudding—I thought it was up for grabs. So I ate it."

"Wonderful excuse," she says. "Just dandy. I was looking forward to it, you know, the whole time getting the groceries."

Liese puts the children to bed with an exaggerated show of cheer and attention in their direction and Johnnie shows his displeasure by not getting up to help. He turns off the television but stays in the living room, reading the paper.

"You could have put the groceries away at least, even if you wouldn't help with the kids," she tells him later.

From there they move to "What's your problem anyway?" Johnnie says she's been acting snarky for days.

"For days?"

Sitting there, paper in his lap, imperturbable, as if he's an accountant and glad to oblige with all the numbers concerning their debts, he gives her examples. Miniscule things, Liese thinks as she hears them, every one of them answerable, justifiable, matters of tone or gesture too slight to count. She rebuts them one by one, and has some charges of her own. His insensitivity. Self-centredness. Reading instead of helping. Bringing a doughnut and eating it just because she hadn't downed it the moment he set it on the counter. Some people delay their gratification, she says, and doesn't he realize the kind of day she's had? How tired she was, carrying the groceries home, the huge bill at the garage? That crazy woman and the vacuum?

"If you'd apologized," she says, "right then and there, when you realized you'd taken my doughnut, just said something like, 'oh I'm sorry, honey, that was yours and I spoiled your anticipation,' all this could have been avoided."

This, she feels, is the truth, the crux of the matter, the pivot upon which everything turns. But he doesn't get it, and won't say it. She feels helpless. She starts to cry.

Johnnie hates tears, thinks them a manipulation. He declares he's going to bed.

Liese follows. They lie on their backs for some time in an agitated silence and then Liese says, tone meek, that she hates ending the day this way.

"Me too," he says. "So why do you do it?"

Her offer of conciliation vanishes at the insinuation. "Me?" she snarls. "Me?"

Johnnie says, "Goodnight, sleep well," his voice brusque and formal. He rolls onto his side away from her and only minutes pass, it seems, before his breath has slowed and deepened and he's fallen asleep.

Her husband's astonishing ability to sleep under conditions like these infuriates and weakens her further. She tosses heavily from one position to the other, hoping he'll waken to set things right. But he doesn't. And he won't. The worst of it is, he'll have forgotten everything by morning. He'll want to touch her but she'll still be hurt and he'll be puzzled by her coldness. "Didn't I say goodnight and wish you well?" he'll say. "Didn't that mean anything to you?"

It's the end of May and the weather is warm. The bedroom window is open. Liese finally wills herself into calmness, into setting the argument aside. She believes there's a space some time during the night when total quiet descends upon the city, some brief space of pure and soundless darkness. Perhaps it doesn't actually exist, but she also wills herself into finding it.

She must have drifted off. Liese jolts awake and knows she's at that point of longed-for stillness. Not even Johnnie's breath is audible. The air in the room is cool and the curtain lifts slightly with the breeze, white and wing-like in the pale dark.

But there had been a cry.

It sounds again. A man calling, "Evangeline! Evangeline!"

Evangeline! The voice of the man in the third-floor apartment, and Liese can hear that he's running, the name flying behind him, a trail of anguish, of fear.

She jumps up and looks out the window. The first cry that

woke her burst out of their building. The next three were sung west by him along Edison. But the patch of street and sidewalk visible to her are deserted.

Now, two more times, the name, like a ribbon floating in the wind. Unfurling behind him as he runs and winding its way backward into Liese's ear.

She thinks the man must be as large as the woman was small. His complexion as robust as hers was pale. She imagines the woman, light and loping, her hair streaming behind her as *Evangeline* streams behind him. She needed air, perhaps, couldn't last any longer in that furnace of a room within the grip of his voice and his overbearing concern. Needed earth and sky, perhaps, and Liese pities her now, remembers how she trembled over the vacuum cleaner. Perhaps she believes there's a quiet place in the warm dark of the silent city too, when hives open and the world has been tidied. When one has enough of everything.

And he like a cat after the little mouse. Caring and catching. Calling for her.

Liese stands at the window for some time, hoping to hear voices returning in the other direction, the sound of laughter or conversation. She hopes to see them pass on the sidewalk, entwined, supporting each other home. In spite of their problems, their differences.

Eventually she climbs back into bed. Traffic is humming again. A siren wail enlarges and fades. A car with music playing blows by. A dog barks.

She wonders if the cries were a dream. She's losing them already, all the syllables of the name Evangeline. The longing they implied, and the danger and freedom. She's drifting away again, not sure what she remembers and what she's forgotten.

What You Get at Home

She remembers how she discovered a book by Anne Tyler, discovered it by accident. How reading that book became a story of its own, like a nesting doll hiding other stories inside it, earlier ones she'd almost forgotten. She remembers how it helped her, how it did the good work a book can do.

It was 1982. She was sitting in the doctor's office with Robert, who was feverish, who sagged into the round wrap of her arm as he paged idly through a magazine, she with her head bowed and looking along with him, each of them a cozy corner to the other while they waited in that spare, white room, when her eye caught on it: a full-page advertisement for *Dinner at the Homesick Restaurant*.

"Wait," she said. She pushed the boy upright. She took the magazine from him and stared at the words of the title. She sounded them in her mind. She rummaged through her purse for her grocery list and on the bottom of it, under oatmeal, she wrote down the name of the book and the name of the author.

She didn't care if it was a novel, a memoir, a cookbook.

Perhaps there was something in it for her. She'd been in Canada a decade already and now—when it should have happened at the beginning, if at all—she was bothered by homesickness. Regular bouts of it, triggered by matters of no consequence: a scrap of paper tumbling over the sidewalk in a gust of wind, the blast of a car horn, an unfamiliar English word. Her heart would begin to race, she would twist round as if someone had rapped her on the shoulder, but always it was only a question that frightened her, a hiss in her head, sounding bitter: Whatever possessed me to come?

She knew the reasons she'd come, she was certain they were solid. A hot, dry, pioneering place, that Mennonite colony in Paraguay she'd left, the place she was born and raised. Isolated. Poor. And growing up she'd heard of other places where Mennonites lived, like Canada, and sometimes people played with the word and said Canaan instead, which was the biblical land of promise. They'd say it smiling, as if they were joking, but she thought there must be something implied in the use of it, some kind of milk and honey, even if they meant to be funny. She wanted more for herself. She'd begun to dream of leaving and then, at twenty-one, bracing herself between the contradictions of her mother—*if I were younger and single I'd go too,* and *how can you, how can you, how can you leave us?*—she did it: she stepped into an airplane and she flew away, leaving parents and siblings and friends and everything she'd ever had of a home behind. And since her mother had cousins in Winnipeg, it's where she went. She learned English and she got a job, and then she met Johnnie and they married and the children came along, two of them. And they were planning for a third. They had a house of their own and Johnnie liked his job at the furniture plant. She couldn't say her life had turned out as perfectly as her daydreams did, but it hadn't been a disappointment either. So why was *Whatever possessed me to come* popping up to plague her now?

She always told herself the reasons, told herself that regret was stupid and useless. This restored her breath, it slowed her chasing heart, but it couldn't prevent the sadness that followed hard upon the question itself, like a hand sprung toward her throat as if to grab and squeeze, as if to choke the satisfaction she had in being where she was. As if Johnnie and the children weren't enough. As if there was something vital about back-home in Paraguay she'd overlooked by leaving, something she'd missed but couldn't see, even though it might have been parked there in front of her.

That evening at supper, Liese reported to Johnnie that Robert would be fine. The doctor had said it was only a cold and time would take care of it. She'd felt dumb for taking him in, she said. If she went to the trouble of doctoring the kid, she'd prefer he was sick enough to need it. Johnnie laughed with the pleasure he seemed to get when she was indignant and then she recalled the advertisement. She showed him the title she'd written on her list. It jumped at her, she said, and she liked it.

"I'm thinking that what you get at the homesick restaurant is what you get at home," she said. "What you're used to, I mean."

He said, "I imagine that's it."

"I've got to read that book."

"Sure, why not?" he said. "You like to read."

Two days later, with Robert better and back at school with his sister Amelia, Liese drove to the library to ask about *Dinner at the Homesick Restaurant*. The librarian told her it was new and very popular and all the copies were borrowed but if she was willing to wait, he could place a hold for her. Liese said she had time.

She'd told Johnnie about the spots of melancholy coming at her out of the blue. She'd called them her episodes of sadness. Now she had another phrase for them, a kind of code. "Looks like we're dining at the homesick restaurant again tonight," she might say, setting supper on the table.

She cooked the way her mother had. Every day, an anchor of meat—fried chicken, hamburger balls, or breaded tenderloin—for even in poor hot Paraguay they'd always had meat, and heaped around it, potatoes or rice or noodles. And spooned over it all, a smooth thick gravy made with cream. Cucumber slices or pickles and slabs of homemade bread on the side.

But she didn't mean the food.

Sometimes Johnnie missed her meaning and he would say, "Looks awfully good to me," and sometimes he got it and said, "Tough day, kiddo?" That was about as much as he generally responded, though once he surprised her by asking some questions.

"You liked it when you came," he said. "You never missed Paraguay then, did you, Liese?"

"Not really."

"When we married, and all the years we were starting with everything, you liked it. Didn't you? Isn't that what you said?"

"I know."

"So what are you missing?"

"Nothing specific, Johnnie." Liese felt tears rising and an ache in her cheekbones. "I really don't know."

"We'll get you back home for a visit," he said. "I promise. We'll get you back for a visit."

Liese very nearly replied, "As if we could ever afford it," but she was too close to crying. They'd opened a savings account for a family trip to Paraguay, but there was rarely money left over to add to it.

When Liese got a notice in the mail that *Dinner at the Homesick Restaurant* was available for her, she went to the library immediately and picked it up. She started the book that evening, as soon as the children were in bed. It was the story of a woman named Pearl—Pearl Tull—who raised her children on her own after her husband had abandoned her, though she always pretended it was only his business that kept him away. The story was interesting and written in a way that pulled Liese along. She was relieved to like the book because she'd been borrowing the title for her own situation all this time without knowing anything about it.

At eleven o'clock, Johnnie emerged from the basement where he'd been watching television. He said, "Hey, Liese!" as if he were calling her. "Coming to bed?"

She lifted her head and also the book, so he could see what she was reading. "I'm not tired," she said.

Johnnie frowned. "It's going to get you down again."

"No, no, not at all!" she burst back at him. "It's not like me at all!" By now she had read her way to Cody's side of things. He was Pearl's son and his version of events was different from his mother's. The story felt more complicated now. And in the table of contents some previous reader had penciled in the names of the narrators of all the chapters so Liese knew that Pearl's other son Ezra and her daughter Jenny would get their turn to speak as well. She couldn't put it down, not yet, and surely the book was excellent, even important, if it held her this tightly.

"No immigrants!" she said. "Nothing like my episodes at all!"

Johnnie stood there a moment, not speaking, and then he said, "All right then. So I'm heading to bed and I'll see you in the morning."

Near one o'clock, Liese roused herself from the story to make a cup of coffee. When she returned to the living room, the steaming mug in her hand, she saw the soft sphere of lamplight around the moss green chair where she'd been sitting and the book lying face down in it and happiness seized her with a jolt, as if she'd put her name in for a prize and won it. She settled back into the chair. The coffee was dark and delicious. Just twenty-five more, she told herself, twenty-five pages and she would go to bed, she really must. She would. She clambered back into the book holding that pledge to herself and as she went she thought how sheltering it could be, like a cave to her, people in a story and how they behaved and the twists of the plot; her curiosity wakened and satisfied. And everything safe and lit with words, safe against the dark and the shadows of the house, but never so bright that it made her self-conscious about how she might look in the glaring light, she with her pale, sweet-potato-coloured hair and freckles.

When she checked her watch again, she was startled. It was half past two. She hadn't been counting and now she'd forgotten where she'd been when she promised twenty-five pages. She wasn't sleepy. She was full of coffee. She could hear Johnnie snoring just a room away. She listened to him a while with affection but she had no desire to lie beside him. Instead, she got up to use the bathroom and she washed her face and changed into her nightgown so she would be ready for bed after a bit more of the book.

She also checked on Robert and Amelia. At each of their beds, she tugged up the blankets and tucked them more closely to their bodies; at each she pressed her cheek against theirs, murmuring "I love you." Her children slept so beautifully. They slept so far away from the troubles of the growing-up children with whom Pearl Tull had to contend. Pearl had said there was something wrong with all of her children. But this was not the case for Liese. The sweetness, the fine quality, of her Robert and Amelia seemed sure and almost palpable beneath her touch.

And then she was back in her chair and the pages came and went and the house cooled and Liese felt chilly so she got up and pulled the green and white afghan out of the linen closet and wound it tightly around herself before sinking into her reading position again. She'd knitted the afghan while pregnant with Robert, in a brief swell of enthusiasm for handwork but it was ghastly, the stitches uneven, not fit to be seen by anyone else. She'd kept it because she'd paid for the wool and it was large and warm. It had some usefulness at least. For reading in the night, she thought, suddenly astonished that she was awake.

Sometime after three, Liese noticed the silence. The snores, the random groans, the tiny cries of the sleepers in the rooms down the hall, the creaks of the house, the wind's play in the trees, the traffic and emergency vehicles at a distance—all had ceased, it seemed, at the same moment. The stillness was absolute. Her heart darted up, pounding in her chest with that familiar, questioning fright. She turned the book face down and pressed her hand over it, dismayed. But she heard her breath against the stiff strong silence and so she made herself breathe more firmly, counting, and while she listened to herself, even before she could haul up her reasons for coming, something she hadn't considered for years unfolded before her like the next pages of the novel in her lap.

She's seven and it's her first day of school. She and her best friend Helen are walking along the packed earth path to the village schoolhouse. She's very excited. Jittery too. Maria, who's going into the third class, is walking with them. Maria has dark hair in two thick braids with blue ribbons at their ends. She's telling the two beginners how to behave in school. She's telling them the rules. Maria is bossy and all the village girls do what she says.

Does Liese want to impress, or is she unable to contain her excitement? Out it comes, as proud as an egg, fresh in the corner of the henhouse: "I already know how to read!"

Maria stops. Liese and Helen stop too. They wait. Has Maria spotted a snake on the path? But the older girl is lifting a school reader out of her bag and opening it to the middle, opening it deliberately and precisely, as if she's dividing a tangerine for them to share. She sidles next to Liese and her finger picks out a line of words. "Read!" she commands.

Liese is shaking and she's confused and she feels like running home but she also wants to go to school and Helen has shuffled close, her arm touching hers as if it might be of assistance, so she reads the words that Maria's finger is underlining for her. She follows the finger for a sentence or two, until the other girl pulls away the book and slaps it shut. Maria makes a slapping sound with her lips as well, as if she's disgusted, as if Liese got the words all wrong, though she knows she got them right.

Maria says, "You're not supposed to learn to read until you come to school! You should be ashamed of yourself."

She is ashamed. But if she can't be sure how she learned the sounds of the letters and how they cluster into words and then into sentences, how could she have stopped herself? They stand there, the three of them, awkwardly, as if the puzzle of this is more than they can solve, and then they resume their progress along the path to the school.

The first three grades share the same room, the same teacher. All that year, Liese will sense Maria's eyes on her. All that year, Liese will pretend she's learning to read along with her companions in the first class and sometimes she makes a mistake on purpose.

But one day Maria corners her at recess. She tells Liese there's something she should never forget. "Just because you're smart doesn't mean you're pretty," she says. "You and your straw-red hair."

Liese sighed. Once, twice, and then she picked up *Dinner at the Homesick Restaurant*, picked up the Tulls where she'd left them, picked up herself as a woman, in Winnipeg, reading. Sometime in the last hour or so—was it while her own story came back to her?—she'd made the decision to stay up the rest of the night, if that's what it took to finish the book. And now, because she'd decided she would, she read onward in a zigzag of desperation and euphoria, sometimes aware of herself in the process and sometimes losing herself for long stretches in the mixed-up, fascinating lives of Pearl and Cody and Ezra and Jenny.

She reached the end of the book just before six in the morning. In the last hour she read faster than she'd ever read before, though she comprehended every word; she was entirely at home in her acquired English language. She closed the book and put her unused marker on top of it, and she got up and went to bed. There she lay on her back, strangely wide awake, overwhelmed by what she'd done. The alarm clock buzzed and she turned it off. She curled against Johnnie and he stirred and pulled her toward him, his body warm and urgent, hers suddenly sleepy, acquiescent, though her mind was still alert, still trembling a little, as if perched on some high and precarious place with the landscape vast below her. He has no idea, she was thinking, that the story is over. That Pearl died and her husband came back. That she—Liese—had been gone all night.

When Johnnie got up, she followed him as she did every morning. She made his breakfast and she packed his lunch. When he was out of the house, she woke Robert and Amelia and she got them fed and ready and off as well. She had a part-time job at the Food Fair down the street, but her shift didn't start until noon. She planned to sleep for a while but first she opened the notebook where she kept track of what she read.

She entered the date, the title, and the author's name. "Read in one sitting," she added. "Through the night." Liese thought about this and then put an exclamation mark at the end of it.

She wrote out the book's first sentence, about Pearl Tull on her deathbed. Then she wrote out the last. It was about an airplane, small and hanging in the air, and "droning" like a bee.

Liese closed the notebook. She stared out the kitchen window at the neighbours' house with its freshly painted yellow siding, not really seeing it but something just as bright instead, the morning light on the long-ago street of her village in Paraguay and, like a bit of old paint flaking away, her own memory of an airplane.

The morning is very hot, the heat pushing against her face and limbs, even through the thin soles of her sandals. She's walking with Bruno and Helen. Henry, who leans against the gatepost at the end of his lane, joins them halfway down the street. Then the boys form a pair and walk ahead of the girls. Liese is wearing a navy dress with a round white collar that her mother just demoted from a Sunday dress to a dress for school. Liese likes the way it swirls around her legs. She likes the slight rub of the sleeve's starched cuff against her upper arm.

She's waiting for Helen to mention the dress, because Helen, though timid, is an admiring friend, and Liese knows it will come, and then she hears a low whine enter the space she's holding open for the compliment and moments later they see what's making the sound, a silvery white mechanical bird approaching from the left. Liese has seen airplanes in pictures so she knows what it is, but the Chaco in Paraguay is far from cities, from the world, and this is the first real airplane she has ever set her eyes on. And then her friends are yelling with excitement and they're tearing down the dusty street as if to intercept the creature flying above them. Even meek, adoring Helen is running, thinking perhaps that Liese is behind her.

But she hasn't followed them. She doesn't want to run, because of her pretty dark blue dress. She can stand where she is—can't she?—to watch the silver airplane's progression over the sky. She watches and wonders if the people who drive the airplane are also watching her. She wonders if they can see what she's wearing. She holds a prim, attentive pose though her hands are pressed against her ears to block the sound. She believes that closing her ears will help her see.

The airplane moves along the length of the village away from her, too quickly it seems, and all too soon it disappears out of sight behind the bush and horizon. Then she claps her hands over her eyes instead of her ears because she doesn't want to lose the airplane's dangling thread of sound. But it's not enough; the low hum floats away and grows weaker and weaker until it can no longer be distinguished from the interminable bird twittering and insect buzz around her. She opens her eyes and sees her friends running and waving and turning in at the school building in the centre of the village.

When they're out of her view, she turns around and walks back home. There's a sandy stretch on the path where she spots the indent of her sandals going the other way. The hem of her dress is swinging cheerfully against her knees. She'll wear the dress again tomorrow and everyone can remark on it then.

Chaco soil is pale brown but it seems especially light this morning, nearly yellow, thin and contemptible, but beyond the green of the bush and trees, the sky is azure and the clouds pure white and rounded and high, and she thinks about how the mechanical bird flew across it and how the sunlight glinted from its fat little body. She thinks of the sound it made, like a gurgle, like an invitation, and how the sound diminished and then disappeared.

Mama is hanging wash. She has a clothespin in her mouth so she lifts her eyebrows to question Liese's return.

"Mama," Liese says, "I saw an airplane over the village."

Her mother removes the wooden pin and says, "I saw it too."

Liese says, "So I'll need to stay home today."

Mama stares at her and her mouth opens as if to speak, and then by some miracle it shuts again and she nods. She lets Liese sit the entire morning in a corner of the verandah, out of sight of her, buried in the deep curve of a comfortable wooden chair that Papa has built for them.

She curls in the chair and she dreams and she wonders and she watches the sky. She wonders where the airplane came from and where it was going. She wonders whether there was room for one or two or maybe even three or four people inside it, and what it would be like, growing up in some other place. She contemplates what she's grasping for the first time, feeling the fear of it and its even greater allure: that people as alive as she is alive at this very moment are living—breathing and thinking their thoughts—in places other than her village, other than the settlement that is her world.

Liese remembers how after *Dinner at the Homesick Restaurant* in 1982, she went on to read Anne Tyler's earlier books, and as new Tyler books were written and published, she read those too. She liked them all, though never as much as the one she read first, the one she'd read through the night.

As for her bouts of homesickness, they lessened and eventually they stopped. And several years later, she and Johnnie had saved enough and they took themselves and the children for a visit to her former home in Paraguay.

She asked her mother then if she remembered the day she skipped school because of an airplane.

Mama replied that she remembered it well.

So why had she let her stay at home?

Her mother waited a while before she replied, as if to consider which one of several possible answers she might choose, or perhaps to steady her emotions. "You were such a strange little bird at times," she finally said. "But I thought to myself, she knows how to read, so what difference can it make, missing a day of school? She can read, I thought, so I know that she's going to be fine."

Something's Got to Give

It's the hottest day of summer so far, heading for a record. It's humid. The air seems stuck to itself, unable to move.

"Something's got to give," Liese says.

Inside, there's two fans running and she has the curtains tightly closed. She tries to keep the kids from dashing in and out and letting in the heat. It all helps a little, but not enough.

It's Michael's fourth birthday. They'd planned to celebrate with a family day at the zoo and then McDonald's. Johnnie has overtime coming so he took the day off. But everything's turned into a zero for her. Michael can't go. He doesn't want to go either. He's feverish.

Johnnie says he'll take the older two anyway, they've been waiting so long; they're excited.

"Good dad, Johnnie," Liese says. She gives him a quick kiss on the cheek. "So I'm staying home, obviously. Maybe it's too hot for everybody."

"Good mom, Liese," he says. "We'll be fine." He kisses her too, a fly-by on the lips.

Liese thinks Johnnie and Robert and Amelia were much too cheerful when they left. They were full of bounce and laughter and not one of them called "Happy birthday, Michael" as they rushed out the door. But the kids like spending time with their father and they'll certainly have more fun without their youngest brother dragging along behind them, slow and sick and blubbering.

Michael makes a peculiar noise when he's ill, a kind of mewling. Like a sea gull. Liese pulls the smaller oscillating fan into his room and sits beside him on the bed, patting his back until he quiets. She sings to him, some of his favourites—"The birds upon the treetops" and "Once in China there lived an old man." By the time she gets to "Happy birthday" he's drifting into sleep. A sputtering sleep, as though he's left her but hasn't gone far.

The boy's long tanned legs are sprawled open and completely still. Liese thinks she could lift those brown legs off the navy cotton sheet and hold them to her chest and stroke them like carved wood, so separate do they seem from the deep-breathing body above them, the restless arms, the hands clenching and unclenching. His mouth is agape. His hair curls onto his forehead and both are damp. Liese blots at his face with a tissue, less tenderly than she should. He's a struggle for her at the best of times.

And at the worst. He's inhaling and exhaling like sandpaper rubbing, half through his nose, half through his mouth, and crust is forming at his nostrils. She wants to loosen it, but it may be stuck to the skin. It will waken him if she tries.

"I don't believe it!" she told Johnnie last night. "I really don't! How can he go and get sick the night before his birthday?" The child's sudden illness seemed stubbornness, a veto of their efforts at celebration.

Johnnie, ever optimistic, said to hope for the best. A night was a night was a possible cure, he said.

But Michael was no better in the morning and now she knows that if things don't improve she'll have to go and sit at Emergency with him, though what good that will do besides keeping her guilt at bay, she can't imagine. She's giving him medicine and they'll have to wait it out.

He's sick too much, that's the trouble, and she doesn't think he's a light-hearted child either. How is it, some children smiling from the womb and others scowling?

"Everything changes when they grow up," her friend Anita told her once. "The ugly girl turns into the prom queen, just you wait, and the whiner is the high school charmer."

"Yeah, well—and if it goes the other way?" Liese was thinking of gorgeous little Amelia. And of Robert, such a good boy, that one, an achiever.

Michael twists and opens his eyes. They're pale and their rims are pink. He looks at her but seems not to see her. He was slightly cross-eyed his first year. The condition corrected itself, but some days Liese imagines she sees it still. She imagines she sees it today.

"It's your birthday, Michael," she says, to help him focus. "Shall we have a little party here? Just you and me? Some ice cream?"

Michael nods and pushes up to a sitting position. He's long and thin and light. Liese carries him to the kitchen and sets him on a chair. She slides it close to the table. She gets the ice cream from the fridge freezer, takes down two of her special dessert bowls, puts a scoop of ice cream in each.

Oh God, the heat. It's not subsiding. It's thickening, the way rising temperatures thickened the atmosphere in the Chaco, thickened it day after day until it was pressed so tight it exploded into storm. She's never seen storms in Canada like the ones they had down there in Paraguay. So bad her great-aunt was killed by lightning, standing in the doorway of her house.

Liese leans into the counter, her thoughts pressing and colliding too. *People think I've fulfilled a tremendous dream by coming. The tremendous dream of the immigrant.—And what's such a dream-coming-true actually like?—Oh, it's ... well, everything's ordinary. Nothing much happens that's extraordinary, in fact, in the fulfillment of a dream. It's just a matter of coming to a settled position.—Yes, yes, I see what you mean, but do you wish you'd not come? That you'd stayed where you were born and raised?—No, I don't wish to change a thing, except ...—Except?—Except that the ordinary is the most chastening of all.—Life, you mean?—Life, of course. The chastening that happens here. Or there. Or anywhere.*

The boy has his arms on the table and he rests his face on them. He lifts his head when she sets the bowl in front of him. The dullness—the illness—congeals. His face is like mud to her.

"I don't want ice cream!" he gasps. His tone is peevish.

She's tried to do her best but there's this about him, this resistance. Disguised as this miserable passivity. As an infant, he was colicky. Every evening, holding him, walking him, rubbing his tummy when he stiffened, *colicky colicky colicky* marching through her mind behind his gassy wails, like a rhythm toy, new from the makers of...

And cross-eyed.

But they're better.—No, they're not completely straightened yet.

"Take your kids to your folks and get away for the weekend," the young doctor on Emergency had said, the last time she went in with Michael. "You're the one who needs the recovering."

She'd glared at him. "My folks are like six thousand miles away."

Six thousand miles? She has no idea. She made the number up.

"Well, by all means, go home and have yourself a cry then. That will help too."

The doctor's nose was bent, as if he'd been felled while boxing.

SOMETHING'S GOT TO GIVE

One of the cute kids, she was thinking, who turned know-it-all and ugly.

"Eat your ice cream, Michael," she says.

She remembers Robert complaining about colicky Michael's crying. He wanted to watch television, read, do his homework. Do something. Anything. He said he wished he didn't have a baby brother.

"He belongs to this family now and you better get used to it!" she'd shrieked at him. And she'd thrust Michael into Johnnie's hands, and gone walking, one angry step after the other until the tension eased and she noticed how far away from home she was. Several miles it must have been and then her good mother resolve returned and she was ready to relieve her husband, hold the baby, hug Robert and Amelia.

Michael hasn't picked up his spoon. The ice cream is Neapolitan and it's puddling in the heat. Liese finds melting ice cream revolting. The pink and brown of it, the can't-keep-their-hands-off-each-other mushiness of it.

"Don't you want it, honey? It's your birthday."

He stares at her. And what's he saying with that look? A whimper, dependence, defiance?

"I don't want it!" he howls in his cracked voice, pushing at the bowl. It slips off the table. It breaks.

There on the floor, glass and ice cream in a soggy heap.

"Oh Michael!" Her exclamation blazes into her hand like a bolt of lightning and she's lifted her palm and struck her boy across the head.

She's never done this before but she hits him again, as if his damp face with its red-rimmed eyes is an obstacle in front of her. He's made a sound, a startled nasal moan, and she's yelling, "Shut up and look at this mess!"

Has she hit him a third time, or is it the movement of her arm that circles round him and lifts him, that carries him to the rocking chair? She finds herself there, Michael tight against her body and she weeping into his hair, and though she thinks he may be speaking, she's not listening. All she can hear is herself and over and over again, "Michael I'm sorry, I'm sorry, I'm sorry."

He's receiving this as he received her hand on him, with tiny acquiescent gasps. Liese stops crying, stops speaking. Her mind feels a burning clarity as if this child has gone old in her arms and she old along with him. Again he has fallen asleep. She feels his forehead and knows the fever has broken. She holds and rocks him until her arm grows numb. Then she carries him to his bed.

She can't bear to watch him sleep so she sets his cuddly black teddy beside him. She can't bear to clean up the mess on the kitchen floor. She can't bear anything but to throw herself to her knees beside the bed in her bedroom. She has no idea what to do.

If there was one thing she hated about the religiously uptight place where she'd grown up, it was *Heuchelei*. Hyprocrisy. *Scheinheiligkeit*. The appearance of piety. Oh how she wanted to get away from that, of which there was so much, it seemed to her, the community small, isolated—insulated, they imagined—from the world.

She's kneeling at the bed and feels herself stuffed between *Onkel* Cornelius and *Tante* Wilhemina. Not her real uncle and aunt, but that's what they had to call them, these elders who were neighbours two yards down, at the end of the street. Every day she passed their place on her way to school. There was an old woman begging there one day, a barefoot indigenous woman, her dress no more than a rag, and filthy, her woven sack hanging over her arm, flat and flapping with its emptiness. Begging in the Low German dialect, using the few necessary words the indigenous peoples had learned. "Please, please," she'd begged, "just a little bread."

And *Tante* Wilhemina, she gave a harrumph as if it was some word she'd learned from the woman's language and the rest of what she said was lost in the end of a broom. A swish, dust in the air, and "off with you!" So what could the old woman do but scuttle away to try her luck elsewhere?

Liese hated *Tante* Wilhemina Neufeld after that, so plump, so white, so rich in brooms and bread. She was her Sunday school teacher, though, and could tell the stories with a flair, as if she'd walked around in the Bible and seen everything there with her very own eyes. It was hard not to be enthralled with her tales but Liese struggled against them after what she'd seen, out of sight behind the mint bush.

And *Onkel* Cornelius, her fifth-class teacher and a preacher. Likes to feel the beans, someone told her when she was in grade school, and somehow she got the drift of that, vague as it was, and kept her arms on her desk, hiding her nipples behind them, invisible and un-bean-like though they were. And later, in middle school, the whispered warning again, the uneasy giggles about how cleverly he could brush, accidentally, against the girls, who had more than beans on them by now.

One evening when she passed their house they were sitting on chairs they'd set close to the street, the better to see who was out and about, she supposed, the sun behind them setting, and their smiles wide as if they were the first stars of the night. They had an extra chair between them, she realized then, and she remembers now that it was a lovely evening, just after they'd had a big rain and the air was clean and cool. "Dear Miss Sawatzky," they'd said, "isn't it a pleasant night and wouldn't you like to sit down for a bit, tell us how you're doing?"

She felt timid in front of them but said no, she couldn't stop, Mama was waiting.

Now she's sitting between them, head sinking into the bedspread in her utter humiliation. Hitting her Michael. They're

smiling at her with the superiority of those who pioneered, suffered, and survived. You're not perfect either, they seem to say.
They're squeezing her between them, a flicking broom on the
one side and a creeping hand on the other. Ah, they seem to be
saying, you're one of us.

She's one of them. She remembers the annual community
preaching services at which the youth were expected to put up
their hands or come forward or do something to indicate their
remorse and agreement with the doctrines, and then there'd be
baptisms at the various churches later, like preserves from the
crop they'd picked off at the meetings.

She'd wanted none of that. She still doesn't. But, it's not the
point.

"Forgive me, forgive me." Not Michael now, sleeping less
noisily just around the corner. She's failed him and all her expectations and every critical bone in her body and she has no good
reason to flee that bunch of hypocrites now. *Onkel* Cornelius
and *Tante* Wilhemina have seen what she's done. She and her
friends laughed behind their backs, called them the pickle and
the pear.

"Forgive me. Forgive me." She repeats it until she feels she's
been heard. Until she's ready to sit at Michael's bedside, holding
his small thin hand while he sleeps.

When Johnnie and the other children come home, they have
a hamburger and milkshake for her, and a McDonald's kid's
pack for Michael. Liese hugs them all but she hangs onto Johnnie, her eyes filling with tears. It's frightening to be converted,
she thinks, no matter where you are. No one should undertake
it alone.

Acknowledgements

My warmest appreciation to the team at Turnstone Press; my editor Wayne Tefs; cover artist Miriam Rudolph; the writing groups where some of these stories debuted; and my husband Helmut and our family. All of you, by your excellence, input, friendship, and support, have become part of this book and I'm grateful. As noted on the copyright page, earlier versions of some of these stories have been published in literary journals. To the editors of these publications, my thanks as well.